at your darkest

at your darkest

a t. jane palmer novela

TATE PUBLISHING
AND ENTERPRISES, LLC

Published by Tate Publishing & Enterprises, LLC
127 E. Trade Center Terrace | Mustang, Oklahoma 73064 USA
1.888.361.9473 | www.tatepublishing.com

Tate Publishing is committed to excellence in the publishing industry. The company reflects the philosophy established by the founders, based on Psalm 68:11,
"The Lord gave the word and great was the company of those who published it."

Book design copyright © 2016 by Tate Publishing, LLC. All rights reserved.
Original cover design by Aaron Paul Wood and Dark Phoenix Productions Digital LLC
Interior design by Caypeeline Casas

Published in the United States of America

ISBN: 978-1-68333-902-1
Fiction / Christian / General
16.06.08

This book is an affirmation of hope.

It is based on actual events and accentuated by the undoubted presences of good and evil.

It is dedicated to those brave enough to bare their hearts to me with memoirs of sorrow, grief and despair.

By sharing their stories, I pray they find solace in knowing that they are no longer bound by the chains that hold them back from experiencing a joyful life.

This book is also for all the unbelievers. It is for the doubters, the disappointed, the rejected and the fearful.

It is for the sinners; therefore it encapsulates *all* of us.

I pray this book helps you understand how easy it is to give up what is preventing you from recognizing the sincere love of God- for only then will you be set free.

Contributors: Your words will surely leave imprints on others and your courage will not be in vain.

Finley Jo-

In your life, it is my job to protect you. Since the day you were born, I fought for you. I watched you cry, felt your pain as you fell while learning to walk, and did my best to console you when you did not understand your troubles.

Many of us fought for you- but *all* of us prayed for you.

We prayed for guidance and love. We prayed for direction and purpose. We prayed that God would harbor you from harm and discontent. We prayed that He would give you the most abundant life.

And I prayed, every, single night tirelessly- that I would be a good example for you. I failed more times than not. But please know that I never once thought about giving up. Not one time.

Often times I would cry myself to sleep, afraid that I was letting you down- worried that I was not good enough for you. I always wanted to give you *everything*- even if I knew it wasn't in your best interest. I simply wanted you to be happy. I wanted you to feel loved- because truthfully, there will come a day in your life when no matter what you do, it will never be enough for someone. You *won't* feel loved. It's not your fault. You *are* good enough.

You will be heartbroken, yes- but only for a short while because the amount of love I have for you exceeds what anyone else could offer. I will always be there for you.

You should expect to have struggles in this life. Others will hurt you and try to bring you down. Don't worry about them; instead, pray for them diligently and understand that God is fighting these battles for you.

And He always wins.

Before you were born, God had a plan for you- a very *meaningful* plan for your life. Believe me when I tell you that He will lead you in the direction you should go. So when you feel Him pulling on your heart, please- do not ignore Him. He is showing you your purpose.

He is leading you and urging you to follow Him.

I am so excited to watch that plan unfold as you grow.

You see, you are a bright light in this dark world.

You are different.

God has instilled in you a compassionate heart, even from a very young age. It is your job to spread your light around. It is your responsibility to demonstrate Christ's love to others, just as He demonstrated His love for you on the cross.

I believe in you.

Here is the advice I have for you: Make time for others. Listen to them. Help them. Give more than you take. Never stop doing what you know is right. Never stop loving people. Be honest and caring and forgiving, for you are called to do these things- especially for those who may not deserve it; especially when *you* don't feel like doing them. This will gain you the most reward.

When you were merely three years old, you had difficulty when trying to wear gloves the first few times. I would watch you struggle and become frustrated until you would finally ask for my help.

I recall the first snow of the season; I asked you to come outside with me so that you could enjoy it. I handed you your gloves once more. And once more, your attempt was unsuccessful. I remember telling you that you would practice until you could do it on your own- that it was just the two of us now and that Mommy needed you to be a big girl and help as much as you could.

And then I observed intently as you took your time and for the *first* time, put each glove on flawlessly. I remember the way I felt as tears streamed down my face. With an enormous smile, you shrieked, "Mommy! I did it! All by myself!" Still crying, I knelt down to you and hugged you.

And then you looked at me and asked me if I was proud of you.

I nodded my head yes. I had never been more proud.

Finley, you must never give up. Never let anyone tell you what you *can't* do. God has promised you that you *can*.

I know you will do amazing things in this lifetime.

Find refuge in Him and He will shelter you. You are never alone.

Love, Mommy

PROLOGUE

I don't have all the answers. I can't tell you how or when- but I can tell you *why*.

From a very young age, I always contemplated the idea of life after death. I wondered if the heaven that I had perpetually heard about was indeed a real place- and more specifically, if I would see it someday. I spent so much time trying to figure it all out.

I had so many unanswered questions: Would I ever reunite with those that I had lost along the way? If so, would they remember me and all the good times we once had? Would I really be there forever? How long is *forever*? What would actually occur in heaven? Would I meet God? What would He say to me?

Would He feel disappointed in me.

I wanted to believe there was truth in what I had been told about the afterlife but my mind had been too closed off. I had gone through so many misfortunes in my life to ever be convinced that something so perfect was waiting for me. Based on my experience, there was no such thing as *perfect* anymore.

Even as I matured and my knowledge of life and its unfairness expanded, I still questioned if this- this fleeting period of time on earth- was all there was. Was I really meant to just exist for a few years and then slowly fade from remembrance?

Was this really all God had in store for me?

There comes a time in all of our lives, usually a dark time, when we go one of two ways; we turn to God or we turn to the *world*.

Perhaps we turn to God because of an inherent and uncontrollable urge instilled in us that demands for answers and explanations. Perhaps we turn to Him in hours of desperation, when no one else seems to care. Maybe this supplies us with the temporary comfort we long for.

Or maybe we turn to God just in case. Just in case heaven is real.

Just in case *hell* is real.

So why then, do we also turn to the world? Do we think it will save us? Or is it simply because it is all we know? Is it because it is tangible, therefore it must be real?

But we often forget that this world is only a provisional holding place. We will not be here forever. Why else would we be given time- such a fleeting period of time on earth- if God had invested so much into imagining and creating us? Why wouldn't He just let eternity transpire on earth?

After asking myself all these things, something would always tug at me, making me second-guess myself; almost like it was saying, "You know better."

I tried to ignore it.

I once spent some time with an old man who was very dear to my heart. We talked a lot about life, death and what happens after.

He said to me, diplomatically one day, "Come. Let me show you how easy it is to understand."

I watched him as he dumped a five pound bag of rice into a large bucket. He then took a single, miniscule piece of rice, colored it black with a marker, and ever so carefully placed it back into the bucket.

"You see? That black piece of rice- that tiny, unnoticeable piece is your time here on earth. And the billions of others? That's eternity. Now you tell me what's important."

His point was very clear.

I will never forget that man. Nor will I ever forget the seed he planted within my heart. He reassured me that indeed there is more to life than this.

You see, I was raised Christian. I sang the songs. I read the Bible. Three times through, actually. I taught the Sunday school classes. I even went on mission trips. I gave to the church. I gave to others. I sacrificed. I studied. I trusted.

I believed in a powerful, loving and forgiving God.

But then He failed me.

Over and over again, I became disappointed. Time after time, I would ask Him to rescue me; to save me from the mess I was in. To help me get *out*. I bargained and made outrageous promises to Him. But as hard as I listened, I never heard a response. I never saw a sign.

I was beginning to just expect and *accept* defeat. I couldn't understand the concept of giving His will complete and limitless reign over my life.

Time went by and I began finding myself slowly turning away from Him. I had made it this far on my own; and obviously He had abandoned me. What other explanation did I have for such a cataclysm of a life?

I gave up on Him and started depending more on myself. I knew I would figure it out somehow. I always had. I always found a way.

I started to believe that *my* will was much stronger than His.

I found myself still praying, however, but only when things were *really* bad. I had finally accepted that I would be left to deal with my demons on my own- and not metaphorically speaking.

Honestly, I never truly believed that real evil was out there or that it could even be the root cause of my downward spiral of a life. I wasn't worried, however, because I didn't think it could affect me. Christians were supposed to be covered by the blessed and holy assurance of God- so surely I was unsusceptible to it.

But my outlook changed drastically when I realized that I was *not* immune to it; that as a believer, I was actually more prone to the intervention of dark forces in my life. I was a *target*. And these poisonous arrows that were flying at me

from every direction were what had been hinder-
ing me from the life I was supposed to be living.

The good life.

Friends, if you don't understand the complexity
of spiritual warfare and the impact it can have
on your mind and soul, please prepare yourself
for this story. It is *real*. It is happening all the
time.

It will make you uneasy.

My sincere and only hope for you is that by
the end of this book, you will have a better
understanding of just how tangible this ideol-
ogy really is- and then what to do with this very
important information.

I used to think that spiritual warfare was a
theory that was simply created by biblical schol-
ars to emphasize the fact that bad and good forces
are ever present and that there are consequences
to the choices you make.

I couldn't have been more wrong.

The spiritual realm is so very certain and battles are happening all around us- even at this
very moment. Don't be alarmed or paranoid by these
thoughts; instead, remind yourself to be aware. We
must protect ourselves.

We must be ready.

As a writer, words and sentences don't always flow as freely as you would like. And yet even sometimes your thoughts come in the form of dreams- and you often yearn to remember them, because in your dream, they are so meaningful and are exactly what you have been unsuccessful at saying on your own.

During the course of writing this, I had such dreams. I had such elaborate, lucid dreams that I couldn't wait to go to sleep at night just so I could experience them again. It was almost like a *drug* to me. Some dreams were so magical and intricate that when I would awaken, I would spend hours trying to remember them. I *needed* to remember them. I *needed* to write them down.

They were giving me a new purpose in life. I now had something to look forward to.

But then there were others that weren't so pleasant.

There were some instances when I would awaken, shaking and terrified. Some of the dreams were so dark and evil that I would be scared to fall back asleep; fearful of the possibility that I would no longer be in control of my own thoughts. I had others spend the night with me in hopes that I would have a witness. I took sleeping pills to help lessen the probability of having another nightmarish event. I would even awaken some mornings, covered in bruises- with no recollection of what had caused them.

I was in the middle of a spiritual battle and didn't even realize it.

I would wake up anxious that my dreams had become my reality.

At which point, they did.

My dreams started to transition from enchanting to alarming. I began experiencing a phenomenon called sleep paralysis. During sleep paralysis, it is suggested that your body can not fully cycle through all the various stages of sleep. The body wakes up during a very specific period of the REM cycle in which the muscles are paralyzed; causing the inability to move or speak.

Yet quite possibly the most restless factor is that the majority of sleep paralysis victims have a common, reoccurring theme: the unmistakable presence of evil. There are depositions from victims of demons sitting on their chests, making it difficult and sometimes impossible to breathe. The documented depictions of these images became burned in my brain and I meditated on them. I couldn't stop researching this thing that was now dominating my life.

Day and night, it consumed me.

Every time I would close my eyes, I would see them. If not the ghastly image of a demon, some other frightening apparition, nonetheless. Never in my life had I ever felt so out of control and so far from normal.

I knew that this was starting to dictate my life and I felt defenseless.

The 'visions' I was having were no longer illusions. I began to see physical *bodies*- demons, monsters and the like, often in the same room as me. They would monitor my every move. I would feel them watching me as I tried to go to sleep. I often felt their warm breath on my neck as I sat at my computer to write.

I heard them *talk* to me.

I can remember every disgusting detail about them; from their faceless appearances to their height and even the smell they emitted. It was the smell of pure *hatred*.

I thought I was going crazy.

So I stopped writing. For several months.

While doing so, these events began to occur less frequently- but never fully stopped until the day I stood in the middle of my bedroom and said *out loud* that I would stop writing indefinitely if they would just leave me alone. I even hid my writings as though the mere visibility of them was encouraging the evil activity.

I was now talking back to the demons. I was complying with them. And I was feeling relieved.

Several months later, my curiosity got the best of me and I decided to try it again.

But the very moment I started to write of the grace and mercy of God, the darkness reappeared- and with a vengeance.

But this time, I refused to stop.

And so did they.

As a believer, I knew what was happening now. There was no mistaking that I was being spiritually attacked for what I was trying to accomplish.

Yet something deep inside me urged me to ignore them. It was almost begging me not to submit to them.

After nearly another year of these unnerving encounters, I realized that this disease was actually debilitating me. My new normal consisted of constant anxiety and paranoia. I was always waiting for something terrible to happen to me in my sleep. It began to interfere with my job, my family life and my relationships with others. I had gone from being outgoing, personable and kind to introverted, untrusting and secretive.

Things were getting worse.

I was indeed losing my mind.

I needed to tell someone- *anyone* but I couldn't fathom how I would ever explain this without appearing deranged. I pleaded with God to let someone else see or hear what I had been experiencing; not necessarily to take the burden off of me, but maybe just so that someone would believe me.

This darkness surrounding me became so prevalent that others finally began to notice it on their own.

Friends and family members approached me about my well-being. They told me that I was not acting like myself.

So I made an appointment with a pastor and was able to quickly confirm what I already knew to be true. He reassured me that these attacks on me were not conjured up by my imagination but were in fact absolute. He reminded me that my words and actions are catalysts that determine what my mind gravitates toward. When I open the door to evil, I inadvertently expose myself toanything and everything that is against the good and joyful intentions of God.

He told me that the demons were feeding off of me. He cautioned me that my constant fear and retreat was giving them power over me.

He reminded me that I knew the truth.

I asked him why this was happening. Was it just because of the writings? Was there something medically or psychologically wrong with me? What had I done to deserve this? How, please- how- do I get rid of them?

After much discussion, we concluded that I had been clinging to some events and feelings from my past that were holding me down. I was filled with anger and resentment. These were my *demons* and they were destroying me.

He advised me that until I let go of the hate and indignation, I would remain a captive.

He told me not to give up on what I had intended on finishing. He prayed over me for God to rid the evil from my life and allow me to complete my story. He promised me that if I had faith and spoke fervently of the truth, the evil would eventually let me go.

And one day, it did.

It was only then that I realized my faith alone had saved me. A burden, once unrelenting, had finally been lifted.

I felt *normal* again.

From that moment on, it became somewhat easier for me to gather my thoughts and focus on my direction and purpose. I no longer struggled with my story. I prayed all the time for God to lead me victoriously down the right path; and the words began to flow easier than ever.

I thought I knew exactly what I wanted to accomplish with this project. But He had other plans.

I began to write emotionally and fight my way out.

And when I reached the end, it was not what I had planned.

But then I realized that through everything, God didn't change my story. He changed *me*.

Everything had changed.

I awoke one day, some four months after my last encounter. I knew it was time to finish what I had started; and to do it with vigor.

In this book I will refer to the bad and demonic spiritual presences as the "darkness". Subsequently, I will refer to the good and heavenly presences as the "light."

Although heartbreaking, most of us are in the dark when it comes to our faith. We are looking for answers and always searching yet we rarely find what we are looking for.

We are lacking courage. We are missing *conviction*.

Just like when we were children trying to fall asleep in our beds, we were afraid of the dark; scared of what we could not see. We couldn't see our comfort- our favorite toy, the door to our room. It was only when our parents turned on our night light that we were finally able to rest. That was our light. That was our *good*.

You see, the dark gives way to the things of this world: depression, anguish, despair and hopelessness. Yet all the while, the light gives way to hope, love and dependability congruent with something so much more than anything we could imagine.

It is that last little thing we cling to when the world fails us.

It is the final *truth*.

Many of you reading this have strayed away from your faith for one reason or another.

Don't mistake this as a coincidence. These stories aren't a choice you made; they have been presented to you because you are meant to read them.

Make sure you take that in.

May you realize that the peace that once filled your heart when life was abundant has never left you; instead, you gave it up. But gracefully, it will always be awaiting your return. God has promised you this.

Please know that these writings originate from the very depths of broken hearts and the crushed in spirit. But when their words poured out of them- while they were still empty and reminded of the devastation all over again- they were thinking of you. They were reminding you that your trials and sufferings are only temporary and that there is still hope.

Finally, for those of you who are wondering if I was thinking of you as I wrote this-….I was.

You see, there is a certain degree of promise and peace that you can claim, knowing that your life is already planned out for you.

I want you hear that. I need you understand and trust that this is the truth. You have been granted exemption from the worry and anxiety that has been containing you. You need to do *nothing* else.

When you finally grasp this, believe that your emotions will change from fear and uncertainty to serenity and maybe even excitement. Excitement from knowing that the battles you are fighting and the trials you are in the midst of- these are preparing you for something so much greater.

God's will is a very simple thing to recognize.

The ones who see it are those who have every right to blame God for their misfortunes but instead realize that it isn't His intention at all. It is simply Him redirecting them and asking for one-hundred percent faith.

He told us it would not be easy.

When I began praying for God to do His will in my life, things started changing for me- dramatically. It was like a light bulb finally lit up inside my head and I began to understand that no matter what I did, no matter how much I worried or how anxious I was- I was not in control. Nothing could have changed my current situation. So why carry that burden, day after day.

I would pray the same prayer every night. I knew that if I did it enough, eventually I'd be heard.

Listen, it was not an elaborate prayer. It went like this:

"God, I have no idea what to do. Please lead me. Please reveal your will for my life. I trust you."

That's it. Every night. The same prayer.

It was simple, yet effective. And it's all He asks of us.

The Bible says, "Cast all your cares upon Him because He cares for you."

Ah, freedom.

This command liberates us from our pain and the weight and worries of this world. Because of how much He loves us- how important we are to Him- He is begging us every day to let go of what is pulling us down and instead, turn it over to Him.

We have all asked it. All of us. "Why is God allowing this to happen to me?"

You see, God doesn't want discontent for us. He wants us to experience the best life we can while we're here; and an even better one when we finally leave this place.

And if we allow Him to do this- if we allow and trust Him with what he has already graciously given us- *we will begin to see His perfect plan unfold in our lives.*

That's *why*.

That's why I decided to make His will for my life a priority over everything else.

In essence, these shackles that continuously bind us to the things of this world come with several emotions- hatred, jealousy, discontent, hopelessness. These emotions don't come from God- they come from the world.

So when you feel as though your life is falling apart around you, just stop.

Stop and listen.

Pause for a moment and remember a time that you wanted something so badly. Do you remember asking God for it? Do you remember telling Him that you would do anything for that thing?

Of course you do.

Now, take a moment and think about what would have happened had He given it to you.

I'm beyond certain that the majority of us would be miserable with our lives if we got what we prayed for. And conversely, we would probably blame God for that, too.

That's what a good father does for his child right? He gives them what they need, not what they want. That's exactly what our heavenly Father does. It's up to us to trust Him with our lives. Once we begin doing this enough, it becomes second nature. And I promise you, the things that distracted you before will become irrelevant.

God's desire for us is to experience abundant joy while we are here. That has never changed. He doesn't want us to be held captive by the things of this world and the worries that are beyond our control. He wants to redeem us.

So how do I know this for sure?

Because I see it every day. Maybe not with my eyes, but with my heart.

I see what He did for me when I had nothing left. I no longer blame Him for my past. It took a while, but He knew that when I had lost everything, I would finally turn to Him. I would have no other option. And it's my fault that it came down to that. I should have prayed for His will a long time ago, but I decided to follow my own. Look at how much time I wasted. Look at how much more joyous my life could have been.

Once your eyes have been spiritually opened, it becomes very clear to see His plan for you. How unclouded your disillusion will become.

How full your heart will be.

Even when you turned away from Him, still He remained.

When you felt as though you were undeserving, He encouraged you.

And even when you thought that He wasn't there for you when you needed Him the most, my friend— He had assuredly been there all along.

He loved you at your darkest.

"He has sent me to bind up the brokenhearted, to proclaim freedom for the captives and release from darkness the prisoners."

Isaiah 61:1

It is the powerless feeling you get when someone betrays you so terribly that you use the word "hate" over and over again, without discretion.

It begins to roll so easily off your tongue.

It is the first real heartache. It is the abandonment, disbelief and deception.

It is the bitterness.

It is the hurt, the loneliness, the anguish, the insecurity, the rivalry and the stubbornness.

It is the relapse after an addiction. It is the weakness that devours you. It is the act of self-destruction.

It is the being out of control.

It is the disease, the fatigue, the rage and aggression, the judgment, the denial. It is the depression and the restlessness.

It is the final straw.

It is the relinquishment after questioning your own faith. It is the injustice and the mercilessness.

It is the jealousy and the disappointment.

It is that inevitable feeling that although you have everything you've ever wanted, something is still missing.

It is the emptiness.

It is the moment you are convinced that you are on your own. It is the anxiety. It is the unknown.

It is the rejection.

It is the inability to escape from your past, no matter how hard you try.

It is the regret.

It is the moment you consider surrendering and the instant you finally decided to give up.

It spreads throughout you, leaving you defenseless.

It is everything that's holding you back.

It is the *cancer*.

There was so much on my mind that day.
I never even heard the brakes squeal.
I never heard the loud honking of the horn.

Life had never really been easy for me.

Everything I had ever wanted was always just barely out of reach. I could see it all but could never quite capture it.

Nothing I did was enough. No matter how hard I tried, nothing worked. Nothing sufficed.

Don't get me wrong. I never wanted pity. I never needed sympathy. It was just that I was alone in the hopelessness. I felt like a bystander; always watching my world deteriorate in front of my own eyes. I was losing everything I had worked so hard to earn.

I didn't know where to turn.

Where was the fairness? I often wondered.

As I pedaled my bike slowly down the street, wet from a recent, light snow, I started blaming God for all of it. I had been faithful to Him my entire life so where was He when I needed Him the most? I believed in Him. I knew that He wanted the very best for me in my life. The Bible had even told me so.

So why had He given up on me.

I began to pedal faster as I thought about my place and purpose in this world- but I kept coming up empty-handed. I was drowning in my own self-pity.

I was living my life by the book. I was honest and loving and caring. I treated people kindly. I was compassionate. I didn't judge.

So why. What did I ever do that was so wrong. Did I really deserve all this? I began to cry tears of confusion. I needed answers. I felt the bitterness begin to boil inside me.

The snow began to fall again, lightly around me.

Out of nowhere, I saw the blurred image of a pickup truck barreling toward me from the corner of my eye. I was able to let one last gasp escape from my mouth.

I don't know what happened next. For a very brief moment in time, I was in complete darkness. Nothingness. *Stillness*. My life never flashed before my eyes. I never saw a bright light nor did I feel my soul leave my body. I was just *there*.

I couldn't tell my body apart from my mind.

When the cloudiness started to dissipate, I was able to detect a very faint ray of light shining down on the ground beside me. Ground. Soft. Grass. Not wet pavement.

Where *was* I?

I then heard a tiny bell, no louder than a dinner bell, from far off in the distance. It was ringing a sweet melody that I swore I had heard before. The bell was consistent; it was never off beat and the sound it made was perfect every time.

I didn't know if I was dead or alive.

After some time, the ringing got louder. I strained to find its origin. I held my breath as I listened, trying to locate it.

I remember struggling- grappling onto the ground, my hands and arms shaking from trying to just hold on to something. It took all my strength, but somehow I eventually managed to sit up slowly and steady myself. My head was spinning. Nothing made sense.

I had been sleeping. This was all a dream. It had to be. I would wake up soon.

It was all just a bad dream.

I sat there for a minute or two- actually, I'm not sure how long- until I decided that I must find the source of the ringing. It was almost like it was beckoning me to find it. It was almost as if it was ringing a song that was written just for me- just for this occasion.

Somehow I found the energy to stand, still quivering- and I began walking in the direction of the song.

I walked for what felt like miles. Days.

I was so tired, so confused. I looked around for anything familiar but I found nothing.

Until I saw it.

I saw a vision of an older man sitting in a luscious garden that seemed to have just appeared out of nowhere. As I made my way to him, I realized it was not a vision at all. The man was *real*. He was sitting cross-legged but was hovering about two inches over the ground.

I rubbed my eyes harshly, trying to desperately wake up.

It was hard to describe the man. He was old yet his dark, brown eyes looked so youthful. His face appeared stern but caring at the same time. There was a familiarity about him- as if I had known him my entire life, although I was fairly certain I had never met him before.

I hadn't ever met him, right?

The man just sat there- so still- ringing the bell over and over, so methodically.

I slowly and cautiously bent down in front of him, as not to startle him. He did not flinch.

So much time had gone by. When the old man finally looked up at me, I had never been more mesmerized. I was watching my life, my young life and the recent event that had just transpired- play out like a movie in his eyes.

The only sounds I could hear were the orchestration of the bell, the screeching truck tires and my heart beating out of my chest.

The old man never blinked or looked away from me. In fact, he never moved at all.

Was this real? I kept thinking. Maybe it wasn't a dream. Maybe it was just a mirage.

I became increasingly scared and dazed. I wanted him to stop. I wanted him to say something to me. Anything.

But the man simply continued ringing the bell. Over and over.

Without averting our gazes from each other, I watched horrifically as the final scene of my death played out- until my very last breath.

As I witnessed myself die in the old man's eyes, I felt tears pour from my own.

"Am I dead!" I screamed at him with an anger I had never heard escape me before.

I was sobbing uncontrollably now. Every part of me was shaking.

I screamed again as I got just inches from his face. "AM I DEAD!" I put my hand on his shoulders to shake him but instead *it went through him*. I gasped and stumbled backward as I lost my balance- nearly falling to the ground.

I glanced down at my hands.

I could see right through them.

Suddenly, the bell stopped ringing. The old man looked back down at his lap.

Then, in what seemed like an instant, I felt something comparable to a hard fall; my limp body lying on the wet pavement. My heart was still pounding so quickly that it felt as though I was being stabbed.

I began to hear muffled voices but could see nothing. My body was numb now.

Why couldn't I see!

My breaths were becoming more and more labored and I could no longer keep my eyes open. With every effort, I tried to open them as they began to close on their own, but they were heavy weights that I could not control.

The air was cold and damp on my skin and I lie there shivering as I tried to make sense of what was happening to me. I knew this had to be a dream.

Several minutes later, I somehow managed to open my eyes slightly. Though my vision was beyond impaired, I noticed snow slowly falling on me- big, ornate, soft flakes- the kind you caught on your tongue when you were a child.

My thoughts wondered back to a time when I was eight or nine- lying in much deeper, early winter snow in the backyard. I was lying there, shrouded by soft white- only focusing on the snowflakes landing on my face. My mother was calling to me to come in but she knew I wasn't ready. So I stayed there, smiling, breathing the cold air deeply into my lungs. Everything was perfect.

Violently, my thoughts shifted back to my grim, current situation.

Suddenly, I felt what appeared to be claws, animal claws almost, ripping down the front of my chest and stomach. The numbness from my body quickly turned to warmth. The pain was indescribable. I wanted to scream in agony but I couldn't make a sound nor could I move.

"I'm DYING!" I screamed inside my head. I'm dying. I was *dying*.

Sometime later, I was finally able to force my eyes *completely* open, only to reveal a figure- a demonic, black figure hovering over me, nearly slaughtering me with his razor sharp claws. I heard him laugh this hideous, evil laugh. I was lying there- *dying*- and he was *laughing*. I would never forget that sound. His eyes were glowing a sickening shade of red.

And then I felt his serrated teeth lacerate my stomach. I screamed in agony as my entire body shook violently once more. The pain was so intense that I tried holding my breath in hopes of passing out.

The demon's tortuous mouth was gaping open just inches from me, revealing rows and rows of jagged, gnashing teeth covered in bright red blood. *My* blood.

My blood.

The grotesque demon was clothed in black scales that were sharp as knives. I know this because I felt the weight of his muscular body above me- and his claws like broken glass slicing through my chest, attacking me with great force. He must have seen the terror in my eyes, because his next move involved gashing a long claw into my left eye. I turned my head and vomited from the pain, only making the demon angrier.

I prayed for death. I wanted to die. I wanted this to end.

I knew I was going to die because I had seen it play out in the old man's eyes just a few short moments ago.

"Please, God. Hurry," I whispered with labored breaths. I wanted this to be over so badly. I began to feel light-headed as the blood continued to flow from my wounds. I remember somehow turning to my side and vomiting once more only to hear the wrath of the monster. He hissed so loudly in my ear that I could no longer hear from it.

Still unsure as to how I found the strength, I focused harder on the demon with my one working eye. As my body shook from the trauma, I began to pray aloud for God to end this for me.

"Please!" I screamed to Him. "Stop this!" My own voice sounded muffled. I began to wonder if I was even audible at all.

The demon threw his head back, cackling at me in delight.

I cried at the top of my lungs. I begged God to let me die. I pleaded with him to take the pain away. I cried to Him for relief.

"I give up!" I finally screamed at my attacker. "Take me!" I choked out as I felt the blood move up my throat.

Gradually, I began to see a white light form all around the hideous demon. The light was abundant but I was still unable to make out what it was, where it came from. It was a warm light; and almost comforting in this heinous moment. Suddenly, the demon was jerked from me, as if he were being pulled by some other force.

"NOOO!" I heard him shriek. The sound was so piercing. I wanted to cover my ears but I was still motionless.

I sensed rustling and fighting of some sort. It was frantic, chaotic. And then I began to make out more white presences. The demonic creature ripped his claws into my stomach one last time, jolting my body with a pain so sickening.

And then he was gone. Just like that. It was as if he had simply disappeared into thin air. Though my hearing was predominantly gone, I remember undeniable silence. I remember a serene feeling.

I closed my remaining eye in relief, as I allowed my body to rest. It was over. I waited as I thought about how intense the next few moments would be. I knew I was about to die. I thought of nothing but that fact. I lie perfectly still, waiting to experience what was about to come.

I tried to focus on just breathing. I knew what was about to happen.

I also knew the damage he had done to me was enough- I knew the end was near for me. The pain I felt was proof that these were some of my last moments on earth. Finally, I was able to gather a few brief thoughts. I thought about my family and friends. I thought about my daughter. The tears burned my eyes as they flowed from them. I felt the blood flow from my body- the warmth of it consumed me.

I lie there, waiting. Waiting for everything to go black. I'm not sure how long it took. I was so scared. I felt so alone. Time was standing still. My breaths were fewer and far between now and I wondered how many more I could count until everything just stopped.

One....two.....three....four.

I slowly opened my eye once more as I felt a warm, gentle hand on my cheek.

"She's ready," I heard a male voice say softly.

There were thousands of them. Everywhere.

Demons.

They were chained to each other; bound tightly by shackles to the cold, moist, stone walls. They were gnashing their teeth at eachother violently with nothing but hatred in their eyes. I stood there, perfectly motionless in horror- and cringed as they screamed the most vulgar words I had ever heard. I tried covering my ears but their voices pierced me and I could not ignore them.

There were so many of them that they were stacked and climbing on one another. From time to time, they would attack one another; one demon's sharp claw would impale another. The painful shriek from the victim would propagate a gory fight amongst them. The demons were merciless- even trying to kill their own. The gruesome soene was branded in my brain.

Some of the demons would charge me, only to be fiercely snapped back into their positions by their short chains. This would only derange them more. They would sneer at me, their mouths open, anticipating their strike on me at the first opportunity.

With each challenge, I found myself backing closer and closer to the opposite corridor wall.

When the demons would see my reactions, they would howl in delectation. My vulnerability appeared to entice them.

My mind and heart were racing. This isn't real, I told myself. Just keep going. The hall was long and narrow and there seemed to be no end in sight. The faint ambiance from the occasional torch would barely illuminate the path.

It was the most horrendous display I had ever witnessed. There were demons as far as I could see. They had no pride; some were covered in their own blood, feces and vomit; many of them scratching at their own scaly skin- drawing drops of blood onto the hard, cobblestone ground. Some were lurking in the shadows, but most of them were making their presence known as I hurriedly continued on, trying my best to stay in the shadows, unnoticed.

Although they were disgusting to the eye, I still found them spellbinding. It was hard to look away once your eyes met; their gaze would grab you and not let go. They were most intricate- dark, mysterious colors. They came in every shape and size. Some displayed short, jagged teeth, while others more frightfully exposed their large, razor sharp teeth that would surely shred anything that came near. Their claws could certainly destroy a person with a single strike. The jagged tips of their serrated tails would undoubtedly mangle anything in proximity.

Looking at them, I was convinced they would kill me if given the chance. I feared I would not make it out of wherever this place was.

Closely in front of me, I vaguely made out the shadow of a young man, dressed in dark clothing. From what I could see, he appeared to be my age. He glanced over his shoulder at me and I could tell that his eyes were dark and kind. I was somewhat relieved to see something other than these monsters in the middle of the unknown place. I ran ever so quickly to catch up with him.

The young man turned and acknowledged me, motioning me to keep following him. "Keep your head down," he instructed very quietly. His voice was calm yet directive. Somehow, I knew to trust him.

We made our way past the demons, being spat on and cursed at. I felt them staring at us. Mocking us.

This isn't real, Elizabeth. I reminded myself again. Don't stop now.

I continued pursuing the man closely and kept my head down, just as I had been instructed. I moved quickly and with purpose through the cold corridor, jumping over piles of stagnant water and what appeared to be more blood on the battered ground below my feet. His pace was brisk now- almost a jog. I didn't know who this man was but he was all I had. Occasionally he would look at me over his shoulder and nod his head, encouraging me to stay focused.

In my rush, I tripped over something and forcefully fell to the ground, hitting my head on the jagged stones of the dungeon floor.

When I came to, I saw three, no- four, demons lunge toward me once more, hissing and screaming at me- mere inches from my face, determined to devour me.

I screamed but no sound left my mouth.

Instinctively, I quickly jerked my head back, somehow avoiding their brutal attack.

The man had finally noticed my distress and began running toward me. With one swift move, he picked me up in both arms and carried me away from the monsters who were still laughing at me. I closed my eyes and tried my best to calm my breathing.

I thought this was just a nightmare until I opened my eyes, looking into the young man's eyes from this new perspective.

I knew him.

I just had to figure out how.

He looked back at me with his dark brown, sullen eyes. "They can never break free," he assured me. After a few minutes of carrying me to a safe distance away from the demons, He put me down carefully but did not let go of my hand.

Yet mere moments later, I found myself entranced again; transfixed on one of them-unable to release my gaze from its inviting smile. It cocked its head at me and stared deeper and deeper into my eyes, its provocative grin growing.

I stood there, fascinated, as I watched the demon discreetly look around the corridor and then slowly and purposefully slip its small, scaly arms out of the metal cuffs- placing them down gently and quietly on the stone ground, as not to make a sound.

It didn't look like the other demons. It looked almost innocent- staggering toward me as if it was in distress. Its expression turned from charming to worrisome. It appeared so pitiful and helpless.

I was hypnotized by the demon. I calmly let go of the man's grip on my hand as I assured him I was fine. He gave me a sideways glance but reluctantly let go of my hand. I felt myself walking toward the demon, who was now staring into my eyes with such captivation.

He needed me.

As I got closer, the demon never took his eyes off me. In fact, he continued to look deeper into me- as if he was searching for something. He raised a small, frail finger, stained with blood- and motioned me to come to him.

I never took my eyes of his as I walked closer. Drops of blood fell from his mouth as he extended his hand to me, smiling once again.

I unconsciously reached for it.

I screamed as something grabbed me violently around the waist and away from the demon.

The demon's eyes immediately turned a solid, opaque black and he darted violently toward me- but a sudden, bright light acting as a wall, appeared between us and the demon was unable to penetrate it.

I was shaking as the young man turned me around quickly and clutched my face in his hands while he opened my eyes wide with his fingers and studied them. After a few moments, he let go and sighed a sigh of relief as he shook his head.

"Don't look at them again," he demanded of me. "Or you will become one of them."

I felt the hairs on the back of my neck stand up.

My heart never stopped racing. I did my best not to make eye contact with the monsters as we went on. The path was long and I saw no end in sight. The man had gone on ahead; leaving me to catch up. I don't know how I knew in which direction to go; I just kept going. I felt as though I was in a trance.I was so short of breath. I was still so confused.

The long, agonizing journey finally came to an end. The young man had been waiting for me beside a large set of double doors, barricaded by large locks and metal bars. When I met him, he withdrew a large key from his back pocket.

I watched in awe as the key floated above the palm of his hand, turned once clockwise and then fell back into his grasp.

The majestic doors opened on their own, revealing a warm, comforting light.

The mysterious man took my hand gently and guided me in. "This way," he instructed, as he closed the doors behind us.

A surreal feeling encompassed me as I walked into the small room. I can't accurately describe it. It was as if I had been there before. I couldn't understand why I had felt so much familiarity so many times since I had arrived here.

Wherever 'here' was.

I looked around the room as I counted eleven others. I was the only female.

Their faces reflected mine; unsure of what had just happened, how they got here- but more speculative of what was occurring next. The young man took my hand again and led me to the end of the second row. There were no chairs; nowhere to sit- but oddly enough, my legs weren't tired from the strenuous trip here. Even after all of the events I had just gone through, I wasn't even slightly fatigued.

Why wasn't I tired?

I suddenly recalled the horrific attack from earlier.

I closed my eyes as I anxiously laid a hand on my abdomen and drew it back slowly.

Dry.

I forced myself to open my eyes.

I saw no blood.

There was no evidence of any combat at all. My clothing was intact. I could see and hear just fine.

My head was spinning now.

—

When I was able to regain some composure, I turned my eyes upon the young man whom I can only imagine, had saved me somehow.

I watched him and his peculiar stature as he seemed to glide to the front of the room. It fell silent as all gazes were upon him.

I was mesmerized by his presence. He was dressed like the rest of us but there was something so divergent about him. He looked much different in the ambiance of the room. His dark, brown hair disheveled somewhat, and he had a more youthful appearance than what I had noticed before.

I couldn't shake the feeling, however, that I had met him somewhere before.

Then as I stood there, trying to figure it all out, I watched in awe as a pair of enormous wings, once hidden from sight, began to slowly unfold behind him. They took up nearly the entire platform he was standing on, at least five feet on each side. I tried refocusing my eyes. Was I really seeing this? My arms were covered in goose bumps.

He cleared his throat.

"Welcome," he said kindly. The stern expression on his face softened and he smiled at the small crowd. "My name is Remy." His regard toward us was gentle and compassionate.

He waited a moment and then went on. "Nothing that I am about to explain will make any sense to you right now. But I still must try. Believe me when I tell you that I understand what you are thinking and feeling. I can identify with your confusion."

He paused again, expecting a reaction from the crowd, but we were all hushed and motionless.

"All of you are here for a very important purpose. I know you are troubled- but let me resolve your uncertainty. I can assure you that you are about to become a part of the most sacred thing…" He paused and looked down. "The most sacred of… everything." His voice cracked.

"It is true what your mind is telling you. This is not a dream. This is the most real thing that will ever happen to you."

I stared at him, so lost. So unbelieving. What was happening?

"This is the beginning of eternity for you."

I felt tears pour from my eyes without control. I had been holding my breath.

"Your journey here was beyond easy, I know. And I am sorry for that I cannot discharge the pain of what you felt or experienced along the way. But I can promise you that something beautiful is waiting here for you."

Again, Remy looked at each of us. I diverted my eyes when he looked at me. I felt ashamed and undeserving.

I felt a small urge to look back up. "You are all here to carry out the perfect plan of God," Remy said, staring only at me.

I felt myself start to tremble.

"And this?" he declared, as he held out his arms to both sides, extending his majestic wings- "This is your beginning."

My heart sank as I tried to make sense out of his words.

What did this mean? How? Why? The questions flowed from my mind. I looked around the room. The others in the room appeared to be experiencing the same baffled reaction.

This can't be happening. This doesn't look like heaven. What is going on here? I kept asking myself over and over as if I would eventually get a clear answer.

Remy started to read my mind.

"It's true. What your heart is telling you…is true." Remy stared at the crowd for emphasis.

This is heaven? I thought to myself. And am I an….*angel*?

This can't be.

When I looked at Remy, he was already looking at me. "Yes," he said. I swallowed. How did he know what I was thinking?

"I am certain you are all wondering where you go from here. And what "here" is. What this means, what is about to happen."

He stepped down from his platform and walked slowly amongst us; his large wings now slowly tucking themselves away.

"Each and every one of you were chosen. Whether you like it or not, for the rest of eternity, you have a duty that will never completely be able to be fulfilled without your complete dedication.

It will exhaust your heart and it will break you down. Often. At times, it will even defeat you. Again, I'm sorry for what it took to get you here, but you will soon understand its necessity. You will have many sleepless nights, heartaches and tearful days."

What was happening.

"But," Remy continued as he made his way back to the front of the room, "In return, God has promised you something miraculous. You are healers. You are givers. You are forgivers. You will provide hope, happiness and love. You will witness extraordinary things. You will feel peace knowing that God has entrusted in you the ability to give someone a second chance."

I still felt so out of place.

"You will witness the most miraculous and beautiful things here. You will see your children grow, and their children, and their children. You will see time pass and also stand still. You will literally witness... eternity."

Although I was still so distracted, I felt myself smile for this first time since the accident.

"You will soon learn to appreciate why you were chosen for this. It may take years, or hundreds of years. But the time will come and you will realize that your purpose here is far greater than anything you could have accomplished on earth.

Time is not linear here," Remy continued. "There *is no* time. You can sense something has passed, but you'll never be able to comprehend what it is. This is probably going to be the most difficult concept for you to grasp.

You won't be able to differentiate the past from the future. As far as you know, you've been here forever and as soon as you've grasped that, another eternity has already passed.

There is no end to eternity, of course. It is a feeling, not a time. Not an event. You are simply, here. You always have been."

Remy paused briefly while he made his way back to the front of the room; his massive wings unfolding themselves from behind him once more. No one spoke, although I could tell there was so much discomfort.

"From now on," Remy continued, "God's will is a very important part of you. Waking and sleeping, you will follow it. You will no longer experience doubt or discernment. You will feel Him lead you and you will soon naturally adapt to His guidance wherever you go. If He urges you, follow that urge. If not, walk away."

I saw others nod in congruence. I was still trying to figure out what had just happened. I felt like a huge piece of this puzzle was missing.

"You will also be renamed," Remy continued. "There is no longer a reason for you to be connected to your old, earthly lives. The 'life' you are about to experience from now on is far more meaningful."

Remy smiled warmly at the crowd. "But please don't mistake this. Nothing is containing you here. You are *free*. If any of you feel as though you can't do this, or that you were chosen by mistake, please step forward now." He grinned as though he knew none of us would be so daring.

Impulsively, I felt myself wanting to leap to the front of the room. Everything I had ever wanted was waiting for me on earth. If I could just leave and try it again- I would be a better person. I would be grateful. I would try harder.

I wasn't supposed to be here. Didn't he know that?

But my feet were lead weights. I felt paralyzed- I couldn't have moved if I tried. I felt force on my shoulders, holding me in my place.

I looked around the room. No one moved.

"Then it is settled," Remy stated firmly.

Remy walked around the room, handing each of us a small slip of paper.

When he got to me, he looked at me longingly without saying anything at first. I noticed the freckles on the bridge of his nose. He did not look like an angel.

Remy laid his hand gently on my cheek.

I had felt that before.

"Elizabeth, do not ever think that what you did wasn't good enough," he whispered to me. "You must keep trying. Do not give up on them." His words resonated over and over and sent chills down my spine.

What exactly was he talking about?

Immediately, I started thinking about my childhood and how I felt like I had never fit in. How I always felt disconnected from everyone. How I always longed to love everyone, but how I had often felt so alone.

I began reminiscing about past relationships that never worked out. I was mad at God for never sending me someone to love.

I remembered those times of such grief and despair and unbelief and almost instantly, I would feel someone (or something) tug at me; convincing me that I was wrong. That I wasn't facing these things alone. That they weren't meant for me.

But I always thought it was just the voice of hope. An innate feeling we all felt from time to time, encouraging us to not to surrender.

I remember trying so hard to be compassionate and forgiving. But nothing I seemed to do ever had any impact.

I carefully unfolded my piece of paper. It read: "Name: Ansiel, healer to the hurting."

I stood there, stationary- taking in this new information. I looked up at Remy, who was already looking at me. He nodded in confirmation.

With some degree of uncertainty, I smiled back at him.

I never knew my place in the world. Maybe I was never meant to have one.

Once everyone received their papers, Remy purposefully made his way to the front of the room once more.

He looked up from his feet.

"Now," Remy asked of all of us, "Close your eyes."

When I opened my eyes, I found myself in what appeared to be a cramped room in a nursing home; the sterile smell overtaking my senses. To my left was a tiny window, barely open, allowing just enough breeze to enter the room to lightly blow open the sheer curtains.

How did I get here? What exactly was about to happen? I felt extremely uneasy.

My questions did not cease as I inspected the room. To my right was a small, frail body, lying in the bed, covered only by a thin, white sheet. I cautiously stepped closer to it, as not to disturb it.

I observed intimately as an old, black man lie feeble in the bed. His breathing was so shallow that I had to bend down closer to him to make sure he was still alive.

I looked the old man over. His bony face was freckled and aged with deep wrinkles and his hands appeared overworked. His many years showed prevalent on his face.

Death was near for him.

What am I doing here, I wondered to myself.

The man was so still and peaceful. Occasionally I would see his eyelashes flutter or a feeble hand twitch.

I prepared and waited for this darkness to appear that Remy had just warned us about. I was awaiting some type of turmoil or heinous encounter to occur.

It did not.

"They don't know," the old man smiled with his eyes still shut.

Was the old man talking to me? I knew he could not see me. I listened more. I recalled hearing the nurse in the hallway earlier- she had been explaining to the old man's family that his disease was progressing rapidly. It was the first time they had visited in months. Their visits became more infrequent when they first heard the diagnosis. He was gradually forgetting about them and it was almost as if they wanted to do the same.

Perhaps this was why he was talking to himself, I reasoned. I watched him intently, still listening. He remained so still. My heart began to ache.

"They think they do, but they don't know nothin'," he laughed softly, followed by a deep cough that shook the entire bed.

The man reached for a tissue by his bed, spit into it and coughed once more.

I made my way closer to him.

"Yes, I'm talking to you," he murmured as he turned his head in my direction, opening his eyes most gently.

Maybe he thought I was someone else, I convinced myself.

"I can see you. I ain't dead yet," he chuckled, shaking his head.

"Ex-excuse me?" I stammered, as my voice cracked.

"You're an angel. I know," he whispered as he wagged his finger at me. His voice was playful. "You new here. You comin' for me?"

"You can see me?" I asked in shock.

"Oh, yes I can," he replied, as he shut his eyes again. His gentle smile remained.

"That's impossible," I murmured under my breath. I needed Remy. I looked around for him frantically.

"Ain't nothin' impossible, ma'am," I heard him say, amidst another violent cough.

"The people, they don't know nothin'. They just walk around, mindless. Worryin' about money and cars and clothes and things. How long will they last?"

I could tell the old man was talking out of his head. But if he was serious about being able to see me, what did this mean?

"They too caught up in this place! They too lost in this world. And for what?" he exclaimed.

I understood.

"Child, look around this room," he instructed me with his soft voice.

I did as I was told. The man didn't have much- a small framed picture of what appeared to be some of his children, a stack of medicine bottles and some loose change on the table beside him.

Something urged me to walk even closer to him. I felt compassion toward him. I was not sad; but instead I felt anticipatory.

Compulsively, I reached for his hand. He squeezed it gently.

He looked up at me with his dark eyes. "In the end, this is all we have. We are all the same," he said as his lip began to quiver.

I did not understand.

"It's almost time, yes?" he asked me, as he squeezed my hand once more. His voice was so meek.

I watched him as he closed his eyes once more, breathing in and out through his mouth.

The old man smiled to himself.

And then he was gone.

I continued to hold his hand tightly, standing there breathless from what I just witnessed.

Suddenly, the room got warm and I watched in awe as a host of heavenly beings began to form a circle around us. None had faces or wings- I could only make out shapes and hands; hands that were gently being placed- one by one on the old man's body. The images were bright and each one was more perfect and mesmerizing than the last.

I cannot accurately illustrate what I saw next. My heart was still and I cried tenderly as I watched a sheer image rise up from the bed.

It was a beautiful reflection of comforting light and sound.

I could not move. I waited, knowing that I was about to witness something extraordinary.

The figures were now methodically swirling around the bed, slowly incorporating us. The wind they created was strong, but I was not afraid.

Suddenly there came a fast burst of a very bright light.

And then joyous laughter.

When I was finally able to let go of the old man's hand, I found myself back in the same room as my colleagues.

I stood there for a few moments, dizzy, trying to regain any composure I could. I felt so muddled.

The same feelings I remembered from before began to overwhelm me- fatigue, confusion, anxiety. Was this déjà vu?

No. This was a dream. That is the only logical explanation. I just needed to wake up. I needed to get home.

What had just happened? Who was the man in the hospital bed? Who else was in the room? I searched desperately for a rational explanation.

But then I saw Remy again. Same stature. Same position at the front of the room. Same brown, comforting eyes.

"Protectors," he addressed. "Welcome back," he smiled.

I felt as though I was going through some sort of conditioning or hazing. I just wanted answers and they seemed non-existent.

"From now on, the ones you come in contact with are intended for your intervention. You will have two choices- the first one is to save and the second one is to let go."

Let go?

What was he talking about? How would I know?

Save?

"You won't save everyone. But should you, you are inevitably allowing them a second chance at life on earth. Use these opportunities wisely."

Remy continued to explain that from now on, our duties would be to comfort, protect and transition. We now had an obligation to open the eyes of the broken in spirit; either by granting them a second chance, or helping them let go of their time on earth.

"Listen closely," Remy urged the group. "They are chained to their despair, their hurt. You must set them free."

I waited for more clarification, but none came.

"And need I remind you that not everyone will be saved- so listen very closely for His will. Some have been waiting for this day for a very long time," he smiled.

I nervously smiled back at him.

Although I finally somewhat understood my job now, I still had no idea what was really in store for me.

JOURNAL ENTRY

I died today.

I don't really remember how.

All I can recollect is darkness. There was a hallway of some sort and things were trying to attack me.

I think I was walking down the hallway alone, but it felt like two enormous, strong men were walking beside me the entire time.

I never *saw* them. I just *felt* them.

I'm sorry if this doesn't make sense. It doesn't to me, either.

I somewhat remember praying for that walk down the dark hallway to end. I didn't belong there. It took so long.

I don't really remember much more of it anymore. Remy told me it doesn't matter.

This is heaven. I wish I could explain more. It's nothing like how I pictured. But it is still perfect in a very odd way. I can't believe I was always so afraid to die.

By the way- Remy is an angel- a very special one from what I gather. And I guess I am, too. He calls me a protector, though. There are others like me here. Remy explained to us that we are being trained. But for what, he would not say. I just feel like we are being prepared for something big.

I think I am going to be spending a lot of time with Remy.

He has asked me to follow him closely; to watch and listen to him. He promised me that he would not falter.

Remy is in the highest of the arch angel sectors. There aren't many of them here. He is a teacher, yet humbly he presents himself as a servant. I guess he's been here for a long time. Everyone knows who he is. Everyone seems to respect him.

It may sound strange but I love looking at Remy. He reminds me of someone I used to know.

His eyes always appear so sullen, so sad. I can tell that his role has taken a toll on his heart. He appears so conflicted. He is always off on his own. I feel like he's battling something.

I wish I could comfort him, but I don't even know how to comfort myself right now.

Angels and protectors of all sorts halt as Remy walks by, mostly out of respect. Yet he never gloats. He merely walks with his head down and I often hear him praying for the others.

I'm not really sure what's going to happen from here on out. I'm nervous and scared, but that feeling doesn't ever last very long.

I've already seen some miraculous things here- things I've only really seen in my dreams. Things I never thought were true.

I have a new name here- Ansiel. It means 'healer of broken hearts.' Remy told me that my journey here would be the hardest out of everyone.

He said we didn't need to sleep if we didn't want to. But he encouraged us to do so in the beginning to try and make the feeling of 'time' go by faster and to feel 'normal' until we got used to all this. Oh- that's another thing. There is no time here.

Some of the others are out exploring today after our first strenuous day of training. I didn't feel like going. I think I will just stay here and gather my thoughts. I don't even know where to begin.

I'm not even really sure why Remy told me to write these things down. After all, it isn't like anyone will ever read this.

I watched an old man die today. I saw his soul leave his body. I was frightened at first. Before he took his last breath, he smiled at me as if he already knew what was about to happen.

I saw him here today. He's not a protector, like us, but he was walking alongside a small boy in the garden. I said hi to him and he introduced me to the little boy.

He said it was his grandson.

I will try to write again tomorrow. Whenever that is.

-Ansiel

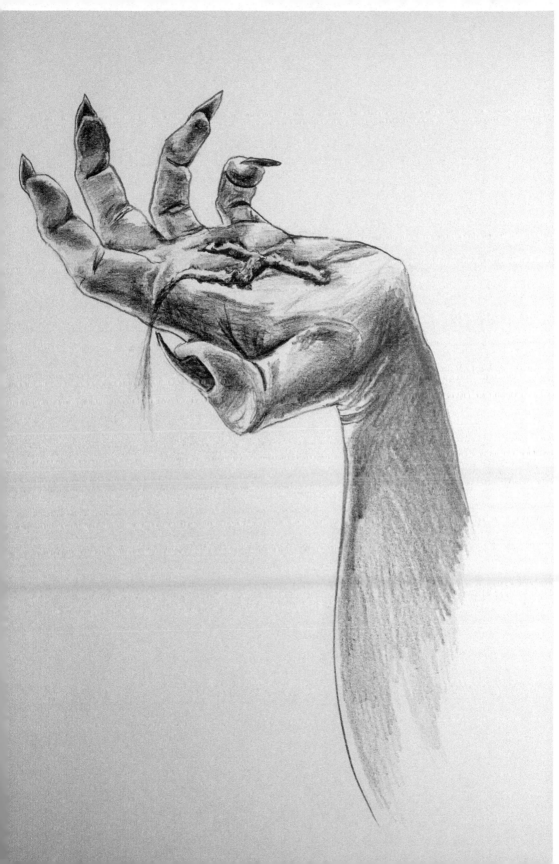

I took a deep breath as I cautiously leaned over her shoulder, reading the words glowing brightly on the computer screen.

"Sure, tomorrow is perfect. I can't wait to see you again. Two days are far too many. And no, she won't find out and I promise you, I will tell her eventually. I just have to wait for the right time. No, I never loved her the way I love you."

My stomach churned as my best friend went on to the next email. And then the next one. And the next- until I knew she could take no more.

"I really miss you. I know this is so crazy- it's like wo finally found what we have always been looking for. But tho timing is terrible. Are you sure we should go through with this? What will happen when people find out? We need a plan."

Amy didn't finish the emails. She ran to the bathroom, vomiting along the way. I followed her, hovering over her shaking body. I wrapped my arms around her tightly. I wish she could have felt me. I should've been there for her.

I monitored her closely as she made her way to her bed, sitting on the edge of it, shaking. I saw her glance at her wedding picture- still sitting on her nightstand five years later.

As she sat there, she drew her phone from her pocket and dialed his number. Four tries. Still no answer. I saw the hurt in her eyes. I saw the new found hatred.

I remained close, resting my head in my hands, defeated. A thick, dark cloud had entered the room from her bedroom door and the temperature in the room dropped.

I waited, nauseated.

A small, disgusting demon appeared from the darkness and made its way to my friend. It stood at Amy's feet- its mouth dripping with saliva- its thin, jagged tail curled up on the floor. Slowly, it climbed up her body, finally perching on her shoulder, hissing words of assurance to her.

"This is not new, you know," it whispered in her ear and it stroked her long, brown hair. "He has never loved you." She nodded in agreement with the demon.

The darkness was abundant now.

Calmly, she stood up, took off her ring that had never left her finger, and sat it down gently beside the picture on her nightstand.

The demon shrieked in delight.

Amy began to weep as the demon consoled her. In her mind I could tell she was putting all of the pieces together.

I glared at the monster, my blood boiling. "She will be victorious," I proclaimed to the demon.

It threw its head back and laughed at me. "She is too weak," it responded, rubbing its scaly, black hands together.

"Maybe. But her faith is strong," I stated calmly in reply.

"Her faith no longer matters," the demon retorted. "She will break soon," he went on, as he continued to comb through her hair with his grotesque hands.

I glanced over to see Remy standing in the doorway with a solemn disposition.

"You may leave now," he said to the demon, in a directive tone.

I saw the demon look up at Remy- a sarcastic expression obvious on its face. "I am finished here," he reassured us, grinning.

Even the demons respected and acknowledged Remy.

The demon gently kissed Amy on the cheek and vanished.

I watched my best friend cry herself to sleep that night.

At one point, I picked up her ring and placed it gently in the palm of my hand, admiring it's beauty and purpose. When did something so holy become something so disposable? I thought to myself. Why would anyone cause this much pain to another? Why the lies? Why the deceit?

I lie next to her in her bed, holding her tightly as she slept.

I missed our good times together. I missed the talks we always shared of our love for our families and how we wanted nothing more to be remembered as good people.

Amy's dreams were heartbreaking that night. Her mind was convoluted with the words the demon spoke to her.

I prayed for solace and peace but I could not save her from it. That was up to her.

⚷

JOURNAL ENTRY

I don't feel like a 'healer' at all.
I feel like I am hurting them.

⊶⚷

Each 'day' here, we would meet Remy for our lessons in the same room as we did on our first day.

And each time, he would remind of us of our purpose.

The room was abnormally still on this particular day as Remy took his normal position at the head of the room.

He looked up at us, slowly and emotionless.

His voice sounded weary. "Even after all my time here, I still wonder why they are anxious. I wonder why they are worried and vengeful. What will they gain? I wish they knew that not every challenge that presents itself to them is meant to defeat them. Their desire to understand and be in control consumes them. Everything they stand for revolves around their discontent and disbelief."

I hadn't seen Remy in this state before. He sounded almost vanquished.

"Soon, the enemy will start diligently looking for each one of you. And he will find you. And when he does, he will try to convince you into believing that you can't help them; that you have nothing to offer them. And many of you will fall for his schemes."

I did not understand.

"You see, evil has more persuasion than good. Evil will tell them that what they are doing is okay. Evil will justify their thoughts and actions."

The others looked uncomfortable hearing this from Remy.

He went on. "The enemy will reassure them that there is no God and no chance of anything good happening to them. The enemy will convince them that we are figments of their imagination. He will try to make them believe that there is no heaven, nor are there consequences for their actions."

He looked down at his feet. "And when they allow this? He is *winning*."

I sat there quietly. I thought about a time in my life that reflected exactly what Remy was describing.

I remember begging and pleading for God to just give me what I wanted. I felt as though He had taken everything from me. I could recall the very second I gave up on Him. And from that moment on, I was vulnerable.

I needed control over my own life. I could count on no one. I really was on my own.

But I still always felt like a very important piece of the puzzle was missing. I felt incomplete.

Where would I go from here.

And then I thought back to a day, sitting in the corner of my room with my arms around my knees, hopelessness overcoming me as I sobbed into my hands.

And then I heard something.

"Stop."

It was a stern command.

I sat still in that moment, waiting.

And the faint voice, once powerful and unrelenting, was now merely a whisper:

"Your past doesn't matter. I've already for-given you.

You may have hurt me before, but I will never stop loving you- no matter what.

The painful things you've said about me did not break me; instead, they broke *you*- and I prayed that you would forget how to say those things from now on.

Just remember that when everyone else leaves you- when everyone else abandons you and forgets your name- I will be here. I will never leave you.

Even when you give up on me, I will never give up on you.

I will never forget you.

Do you hear me? I will never stop loving you."

JOURNAL ENTRY

I often wonder how I got assigned to Remy. Surely there are others who are more worthy.

He never fails me. He never gets tired of my inquiries. He never shows frustration.

Today I overheard him praying for me. He does that frequently, I'm sure, but I had never *witnessed* it before. He was in the garden, alone. I listened for him for what felt like hours.

At the end of his prayer, I heard him ask God to give me courage. He said I would need it.

The obscure shadows in the dimly lit alley were playing tricks on my mind.

They were intent on making their presences known.

They laughed mockingly at me, trying to intimidate me. They made me feel uneasy. They knew my purpose and I could sense that they were here to intercept my task.

I cautiously made my way up the rickety metal staircase on the backside of the abandoned building, trying my best to ignore their threats. Slowly, steadily I climbed. Their warnings grew louder and even more aggressive.

Still I climbed.

The ascent was tiresome and extensive. The shadows continued to follow me; creeping up the brick, inch by inch, foot by foot they pursued me. They were ridiculing me.

When I reached to top of the decrepit staircase, I stopped abruptly and listened. Through the fragmented wooden door, I heard sorrowful weeping. I heard the sound of defeat.

I paused and prayed, as I prepared my heart for my entrance.

The door creaked slightly as I gently inched it open and immediately fixed my eyes on the young man sitting cross-legged in the middle of the dusty, hardwood floor. He was holding his head in his hands.

I focused on him longingly.

I could tell he was once strong.

But something had happened. Something had changed him.

He began to cry harder.

The demonic shadows that were once following me fearlessly on the staircase were now surrounding him from every angle, trying to cause a distraction- but I concentrated solely on him.

"Where are you," he whispered quietly, with exhaustion and despair apparent in his voice.

As he slowly raised his head, I was able to see the tears now streaming down his face. "You used to be here. Why have you abandoned me now!" he demanded.

"That's right," I heard one of the shadows whisper to him. "He isn't here. He never has been."

I stood, confident, in the midst of them as I prayed for the young man.

I watched as his tired body rocked back and forth, his arms wrapped tightly around his knees as if he was trying to console himself.

I made my way over to him slowly and sat down beside him on the floor. The darkness broke slightly for me, but had no intention of leaving.

I could hear the man's mind racing. The voices inside his head were almost too overpowering for me to hear his heart. There was just so much chaos.

One of the smaller demons had taken form now, making its way closer to us. It sat there beside him, silently, rubbing its hands together as if to tell me it was ready to attack the man at any time.

I placed my hand gently on the man's shoulder. His rocking would not subside.

The small demon placed his hand on the man's opposite shoulder whispering affirmations in his ear.

"Time to surrender," I heard the demon hiss quietly. "You're right. He has abandoned you. Why would such a loving God abandon His own child? So sad, indeed." He looked over at me with sadistic eyes while he rubbed the man's shoulders, comforting him.

I closed my eyes and prayed fervently and out loud. The demons were now screaming vulgarities at me. I tried shutting them out.

"I don't believe in you anymore," I heard the young man say softly. "I am giving up on you." The demons' immediate, chaotic choors of vindication erupted.

I looked up from my prayer. "You don't mean that," I reassured him, wishing he could hear me. I knew he was uncertain. So I continued to pray.

The demons were now circling *me*.

When I forced my eyes to close tighter, I saw the reason for his disbelief. I saw the recent passing of his only son and felt the sting of anguish and grief that had overtaken him.

When I finally opened my eyes, the initial demon was now standing between the young man and me. It held its hand out to him. It was *inviting* him.

And then for the first time, the demon began speaking in a language I had never heard. He was melodic, almost as if he was singing a song to the man in words only they could understand. He was stretching his gruesome hand out desperately to the young man.

The young man looked up at the demon and I saw in his eyes that he was succumbing to him. He began to slowly extend his hand.

"No," I whispered sternly to him. I grabbed onto the man with all of my might, begging for him to hear God's will and what that meant to him.

The demon reached further for his hand. "Yesssss," he hissed.

And then I saw the man's son, once debilitated, frail, sick and lifeless, standing in the corner of the room, bouncing a ball off the hardwood floor. A soft light shrouded him.

He looked over at me, with his big, brown eyes and smiled. "He doesn't understand yet, does he?" he asked me.

"No," I whispered back at him, as warm tears formed in my eyes.

"It will take time," the young boy acknowledged. "He misses me. But this is better for me," he said in his warm voice, still bouncing the ball.

"Yes, yes it is."

"I can do anything here. I will wait for him." The boy's smile never faded. The pure happiness and joy on his face would forever be etched in my memory.

I sat there, on the old floor, and cried as the young boy gently put down the ball and walked up to his grieving father whose fingers were now inches from the demon's grasp.

The small boy gently placed one hand on the man's heart and his other hand on his cheek. I saw the man pull his hand back slightly from the demon.

"Dad," he said calmly. "This is me. You don't have to worry about me anymore. Don't be mad. I am happy here. There is so much for me to do here," he said cheerfully. "Dad," he whispered as he wrapped his arms around his father, "It's not His fault. He needed me. And I wanted to come."

I could not suppress my tears any longer.

"I love you," he continued." I tried to tell you at the end, remember that? I will see you soon." He gently let go of his embrace.

The boy looked at me for confirmation. I nodded. The darkness that had once consumed the room was diminishing.

The young boy bent down and picked up his ball. He leaned in and tenderly kissed his father on the forehead.

He turned around, looked over his shoulder at me, beaming.

And then he faded into thin air.

I felt a weight fall from the man's shoulders. He raised his head again slowly and looked in the direction of where his son had just stood. I felt a warm presence overtake him now, just like it did the day his son was born.

He began praying for forgiveness. He prayed for mercy, healing and strength.

I sat there with the man, once broken and crushed, as he prayed for hours.

And when he finally finished, he lie down on the hard floor, exhausted. I stayed there with him until he fell asleep.

Peace filled the room; a peace I am certain he had never felt before.

JOURNAL ENTRY

Today was good for me.
    I finally feel like I am influencing them.
    I'm starting to anticipate more days like this.
    They give me just a little more hope.

"Sit," Remy politely asked, as he pointed to an old, wooden chair that hadn't been there a moment ago.

I couldn't tell if I had been here for a year or a decade. Time wasn't important anymore. As a matter of fact, I was having trouble identifying anything of importance except discovering why I was really here.

I sat and looked around. It was just after dusk and we were in an overgrown forest, bountiful of wildflowers- the fading light of the sun reflecting off of Remy's pale skin. It was just us. I closed my eyes softly as I listened to the harmony of crickets.

I had almost forgotten that sound.

Remy looked deeply into my eyes. "Ansiel, how are you handling all of this so far? How are you feeling?" I could sense the genuine nature of his questions.

I continued to look at him, not sure how to reply. Again, he read my mind. "It's okay if you need some time to think. This is overwhelming to say the least."

I guess I hadn't really thought about how I was dealing with this. "I-I don't know," I muttered. "I am tired. Not so much my body, but my mind. Does that make sense? I just thought it was normal. How is my mind tired, Remy? I guess my real question is… why?"

Remy's smile grew. "Why *you*, you mean?"

I paused, never really realizing that was in fact my question. "Yes," I replied. "Why *me*."

Remy walked over to me and put a hand on my shoulder. "Here is a very simple explanation, Ansiel. It isn't vague. It isn't uncertain. You are here, Ansiel, to carry out the very plan of God, just like I told you on your first day."

I acknowledged him.

"And Ansiel…. It is happening."

I felt chills travel down my spine.

"The demons- the darkness- they will try to stop you. Always. That's their job. They will attack you, and with force. They will never secede. Do not give them any control. They are intelligent, Ansiel, and they will do their best to control your mind and heart. They will do everything in their power to destroy you. However, they won't always be so forthcoming with their purpose. When your thoughts start to wonder and you become discouraged- Ansiel- they've already gotten to you."

I let his words sink in.

"What you've experienced so far is just the beginning. Your mind can only try to fathom what you will witness here. You must remain steadfast. Remember your purpose. Remember what you've been given. This world- this place- they need us. We are all here as part of a divine plan. *His* plan. Remember, Ansiel- you are exactly where you need to be. Ansiel, you mustn't give up."

⚷⇁

As Remy and I stood in the small, cramped bathroom of the home Lauren had worked so hard to make for her family, he gently squeezed my hand and whispered, "I'm going to stay back for this one."

I nodded hesitantly, stepping forward just a bit.

Although my training was still in its infancy, there was no way I could have prepared my heart for what was coming.

The room slowly began to fill with a thick, heavy cloud of darkness as Lauren leaned over the bathroom sink, her two small daughters playing on the floor of the adjacent bedroom.

"This can't be. I'm only sixteen weeks," she whispered to herself, looking in the mirror and then down at the brown mucous on the toilet paper. I saw her hands begin to shake. Her anxiety was rising. I gently put my hand on her stomach, but the darkness had already been there. I saw a small, hideous black demon hovering in the corner, grinning at me.

I monitored Lauren and held her as she clutched her side, cramping. I prayed for the pain to be minimal and fast. I prayed for protection for her other babies. I prayed for God's will.

I followed her closely, my hand on her shoulder as she made her way to the phone. Her hands were tremulous as she called the nurse; the trepidation in her voice was all too apparent. I watched her daughters as they slowly got up from their toys and made their way to her, their big, brown eyes focusing on their mother. The demon that had been in the bathroom had made its way into the bedroom, trailing behind Lauren; its lanky arms reaching just inches away from the hem of her pants.

I glared at it, demanding it to go away. It screeched at me in amusement.

I struggled to make out the first part of the conversation.

"Yes, well actually we've been moving. So I have been doing some strenuous activity, yes. Okay, yes. Yes. Thank you." The conversation was brief.

I guided Lauren to her to bed as her feeble body appeared tired and beaten. I put my hand on her forehead and let her sleep while I guarded her daughters as they curled up next to her until her husband got home.

⚷

I continued to pray fervently for God's will that night, struggling to stay awake; sitting up in the formal chair in the corner of Lauren's bedroom. Remy was still standing in his usual spot- the corner of the room, his arms down to his sides like a statue, his wings tucked away; his emotions never wavering. He hadn't moved all night.

But the next morning would prove no better.

As the early light of dawn shone through the windows in Lauren's room, the scene had become even more ghastly. There were so many of them now; I counted at least ten of them, sitting on the edge of her bed, rubbing their scaly hands together in delight and preparation. Bright red blood was dripping from their disgusting, jagged teeth and gruesome claws. The gratification I saw in their eyes nauseated me.

I stood between the demons and my dear friend. Occasionally, one would lunge at me, trying to scratch at my hands and arms- but would be unable to encroach me.

The darkness in the room had overtaken the sunlight and was now more prevalent than ever. A cold wind blew through the bedroom, blowing the satin curtains open. I looked to Remy but his head was down. I was preparing myself. I knew the worst was yet to come.

Lauren's husband had already left for work, taking their two young daughters to school on the way. My heart withered as I watched her awaken to more blood in her bed. "Oh, my God." She grabbed the pillow next to her and covered her mouth. She was so still. I tried reaching out to her but the darkness was too thick between us.

Suddenly and hurriedly, she gathered some clean clothes and made her way to the garage, quivering. Remy and I followed closely behind her.

Lauren's husband met her at the doctor's office with their other two children. Remy and I had prayed arduously the entire way while we anxiously awaited their arrival.

The nurse came in with countless machines and wires. Her husband did his best to comfort her, but Lauren was having difficulty finding refuge in him. Seconds, minutes of static went by but no heartbeat. The nurse said she was out of practice and went after another nurse.

I could feel Lauren's anxiety rising. I again put my hand on her head, wishing she could feel my presence. The second nurse came in and filled the room with more agonizing static. "Sometimes it's hard at this stage," she said. But her face said what her words didn't.

It felt as though an eternity had gone by. I held firmly onto Lauren's shoulders. I realized I was actually bracing myself.

The second nurse moved the family to yet a different room, trying out a different machine.

When the nurse turned on the machine, there was Lauren's tiny baby on the screen. Just lying there. Not moving. I felt Lauren's frantic mind racing. 'He or she must be asleep,' she was thinking. 'She hasn't turned the motion on yet. That's why it looks like a picture.' I squeezed Lauren's hand ever so tightly.

The darkness was so thick I could barely see her face. I knew what was coming.

I hated this.

I didn't want this job anymore. I didn't want this life, or whatever this was.

She opened her mouth to say, "Why isn't it moving…" but before she could work up the courage, the nurse whispered, "I'm so sorry. I'm so sorry." And right there on the table in front of strangers and her children, she started sobbing.

Uncontrollable weeping. Her husband, who was pretending not to cry, grabbed her arm. They quickly turned off the screen, but it was too late. The picture was already seared into her memory.

I stood there, with my arms wrapped tightly around Lauren, as the next hour went on. It was a blur of tears, questions and apologies. I rode home with her, as she solemnly held the steering wheel, doing nothing but staring straight ahead, tears streaming down her face. I tried comforting her but I could not. It was too soon. It was too much. When we arrived to her home, I helped her get into her bed once more.

For two more days, the three of us sat in a darkness of grief. The sadness consumed her. She cried in her sleep. She walked around in a numbing trance.

You see, I had been following Lauren's heart for years.

She had been steadfast; always turning to God in times of struggle. She was strong. She gave to others. She was fearful. She believed. That is what made this so much more difficult.

Remy had taught me in my training that I would soon be able to differentiate which of those would be able to recognize and seek out the light and which would not. It would become very effortless for me to identify.

The next morning, Lauren went to church with her family. When the congregation departed, Lauren stayed in the quiet chapel; her hands on the back of the pew in front of her; her knuckles white from gripping it. She dropped her head in defeat. And wept. And prayed. She asked God why, over and over. She wasn't angry. She was sad and confused. I sat so still behind her in the pew and I noticed the chapel slowly filling up with light. For the first time in days- light. It was so warm.

Lauren was muted. She had been listening for God but was not hearing Him. Her thoughts were too loud inside her own head that she was drowning out His answers to all of her questions.

She left the chapel feeling lost. She didn't know where to go or what to. She had a long list of things that needed to be done regarding her new home but suddenly they all seemed so insignificant. Nothing mattered.

I prayed and prayed for peace. I prayed and prayed for comfort and healing.

It was very soon after Lauren's visit to the church that phone calls started coming. The news was spreading. Family and friends calling and sending out words of comfort and love- letting her know they were praying for her. People sharing their own stories of miscarriage. Offers of food and to help with the children. Whatever she needed.

I watched and smiled for the first time in a week as her daughters hugged her and offered to brush her hair and snuggle with her. My heart slowly grew back together when her husband would bring her flowers home from work and cook her dinner and offer her words of comfort, telling her that things would eventually be okay.

It was becoming clear now. God was sending the light.

Slowly, over the course of the next week, Lauren began to feel better. The phone calls and emails kept coming- like a steady flood of comfort. She began to feel all those prayers wrap around her like a warm blanket. With each kind word the darkness turned to gray and she began to think that maybe her grief would not suffocate her after all. She was not alone. She was loved. Truly and deeply.

One night, several months later as Lauren lie in her bed trying to fall asleep, I watched her as her two small daughters rested their heads on her chest, sleeping peacefully.

I whispered to her, "You see, Lauren, you are the light."

I saw her smile.

JOURNAL ENTRY

My encounters aren't always full of sorrow and discontent.

Today was actually good for me, good for my heart. It was the first time I had really felt this way in a long time.

Speaking of time, I just wish I knew how long I have been here.

Remy tells me that the purpose of some of my encounters will simply be to comfort the ones I meet. Others, protect. And still others, fight for them.

But sometimes it's just nice witnessing God's will play out in front of them.

I long to see them understand the reward behind their faith.

Remy is letting me go on my own more and more frequently now.

I pray I don't let him down.

Things change very quickly here.

⚷

I thought of Remy as I sat alone in the empty diner. I looked longingly out the window covered in the drizzle of the recent evening's rain as I thought about how tired he must be.

I watched as a young woman about my age ran up the sidewalk toward the entrance, pulling her jacket over her; shielding herself from the rain. I watched for her entry as I heard the loud clanging of the front doorbell.

The waitress seated her directly across from me at the table.

The hood of her jacket covered one side of her face. I watched her curiously as she gazed over the extensive menu. She seemed uneasy. Though I knew she was young, the dark circle and sallow cheek on the visible side of her face suggested otherwise.

I waited.

I hadn't seen this encounter coming. Remy had warned me that there are still flaws in the system. Maybe not flaws, but tests, rather.

Regardless, I was right where I needed to be.

I continued waiting patiently- no, nervously, as a young man with dark, black hair entered the diner, soaked from the downpour.

My body became abruptly tense.

The darkness followed him closely.

I monitored him as he scoured the room until his eyes fell on the young woman at my table.

I took a deep breath.

He slid into the booth beside her- the darkness somewhat subsiding but never fully disappearing from sight. At first, I thought they were a young couple in love.

But then I realized she had been crying. And the hood of her jacket was covering an evil secret.

"No one will believe you, you know," I heard him whisper to her under his breath.

The young woman never looked up from the menu.

From behind them arose a fleet of demonic images. I had never seen so many of them at once- except for my first day here. There had to have been twenty or more of them; all surrounding the young couple. They were anticipatory- as if they had been waiting on this moment for all of eternity

I watched in my own state of panic and anxiety.

The waitress approached the table, but much to her guest's dismay.

"Sir," she started.

"Not now!" he said in a low, stern voice as he banged his fist on the table.

The waitress quickly turned and left as the remaining patrons pretending not to stare.

"You deserved every bit of it," he murmured again under his breath. Worthless. And no one else is going to want you," he continued.

For the first time since I had been here, I felt anger rise up inside me.

His words pierced the woman. I cocked my head slightly as the dim light from the lamp post outside hit her face at just the right angle.

The eye she had been shielding was bruised and swollen.

I saw a single, solitary tear fall from her eye onto the menu.

"Don't you dare forget what I did for you. I gave you everything. You never had to ask for anything!" His voice and temper were rising as other customers began to watch the couple without shame now.

"Please," she begged him, "I know. Please just stop. Not here."

The waitress made another round, making sure not to get too close to the table, but still eyeing the man.

"You know I love you, right?" he examined, as he took her hand from her lap. She was hesitant.

My anger was now heightening rapidly.I knew what he was up to. I saw the manipulative intent in his eyes.

The dark beings that surrounded the couple were whispering to each other.

"How much money do you have on you?" he asked the woman, without deviation.

She fumbled through her purse and counted the bills in her wallet. "Just over a thousand," she said quietly.

He nodded in approval. "Good. Let's go."

She looked over at him with slight reluctance.

"Now," he commanded.

And without delay, they scurried out the front door of the diner.

I cringed as the darkness seeped through the window and followed them.

⚬—🗝

The young couple hurried themselves out to a car that had been left running in the parking lot.

The rain was picking up now.

I followed them closely, keeping a safe distance between myself, the couple and the dark.

They were driving erratically through the small, desolate town.

A few minutes later, the car came to a screeching halt next to an abandoned warehouse.

I closed my eyes and prayed for a deterrent.

The dark fog was so thick around the car. I choked as I made my through it and silently into the back seat of the car.

"What are we doing here?" the young woman stammered, puzzled. Her soft brown hair was tousled and mangled from the hard rain.

"Just trust me," he grinned at her.

He opened his door quietly and came around to her side and did the same. She grabbed her purse from the floorboard and reached for him with her other hand.

He gently shut the door behind her and led her briskly down the dark alley; the only light coming from the street pole at the other end.

I stifled my scream as I watched him pull a small knife from his jacket pocket.

There was no time.

The young woman clenched her abdomen and I saw the horror in her eyes as she dropped to her knees in front of me.

"Like I said, you're worth nothing." He snatched up her purse and ran vigilantly into the shadows.

The sound of the young man's footsteps hitting the puddles did nothing but drown out the celebratory hysteria of the dark images that chased him.

My stomach churned as I ran to her. She looked down at her hand, covered in warm, red blood. She was gasping methodically now.

I bent down slowly and put my hand on her forehead.

"Help me," she begged as I confirmed that she could see me.

Tears soaked her innocent face.

"Shhh," I calmed her, while patting her hair softly and waiting on any signal to save her.

None came.

Emptiness filled me as her pale blue eyes shut on their own.

JOURNAL ENTRY

I don't want to be here anymore.
I want to go home.

JOURNAL ENTRY

I often walk alone.

Aimlessly, still wondering when I will wake up.

I spend so much time searching for those that left before me.

I never find them.

Every time I ask Remy why this is, he reassures me that I will understand why at another time.

I have good days and bad days here.

On the good days, I feel complete. I feel needed. I feel purposeful. I never felt like this when I was alive.

Other times, I miss them. I can barely remember them now, but if I try really hard, I can recall something special about each one of them.

I can't see her face anymore, but I can still see her bright, red hair.

I can't see his warm smile anymore, but I can see his dark, caring eyes.

I don't want to forget them entirely. My heart aches just knowing that one day I will.

Those are the bad days.

I still think this is a dream.

But it isn't. This is my reality.

Again, we gathered.

"Protectors," Remy addressed from the front of the room. "Your strength and your faith are being tested. The demons- they are merciless. Remember this. They are disguised and relentless at times. Do not waiver. And you mustn't give up. They are fighting you because you are strong. But they also know your vulnerabilities.

The darkness you are seeing will only get more and more prevalent the stronger you become. Do not fear it but do not ignore it. They won't give up until they have a piece of you.

But all of you know how the story ends."

I stood in the middle of the crowd that had gathered on the street.

I heard the explosion.

I saw the chaos, the confusion.

I couldn't decipher what was happening but I saw the look of terror on their faces. Some of them saw me.

I could do nothing for them. I heard such loud screams of agony.

The pandamonium was overwhelming.

I continued to stand there, waiting on any indication of what I was to do next.

I began to feel helpless. I was running around so frantically.

There were too many of them.

"Please," I begged Him.

I closed my eyes so tightly, waiting to hear Him.

And just like the last encounter, I heard nothing.

JOURNAL ENTRY

Gods mercy is flawless.

That is something I am sure of.

It is something I see every day here.

The humans, they mock Him. They deny Him. They start wars because of Him. All because they don't understand.

All because they believe more in their own destinies.

And all the while, the potential He has to destroy them remains suppressed.

Remy tells me this is because He is a merciful and loving God.

I hear things all the time from them, asking why He lets these bad things happen, if He is such a caring God. It makes me so sick.

They don't understand that they are the ones creating it.

Sometimes, I wonder why He shows them such mercy. But then I remember that I was once one of them.

Remy took me away on our own today, aside from the rest of our group.

He told me that he was proud of me. He said he would miss me one day.

He told me to pray for the others like me. He asked me to always remember my purpose and where I came from.

I can't stop thinking about his words.

The other protectors had a hard day today. From what I gather, there was a large catastrophe of some sort- a lot of people died. Children, too.

Many of the others missed the lesson today but Remy understood the circumstance. He told the rest of us that some of the things we will witness will impact us so deeply that we may never fully recover. Some of us won't heal at all.

I've seen several of them walking amongst me today and they are so solemn- so sad.

But honestly, I like to see tears in their eyes. I want to see them emotional- unable to hold it in any longer

I need to know they break down sometimes. For when I see these things, I know we are all the same.

9

JOURNAL ENTRY

I haven't had an encounter in a while.

Remy and I have been spending every minute together, focusing on events to come.

As time- or whatever this is- goes on, I am finding myself beginning to wonder if this is really still a dream. Just a long dream that when finished, I would awaken and everything would be normal again. Maybe I would remember all of this. But I would still be okay if I didn't.

I'm having a hard time today. Remy visited me first thing this morning to tell me something big was coming and that I needed to pray for it.

My training is becoming exhausting. Every encounter up until now has broken me down, piece by piece.

I am beginning to wonder how I will ever be complete again. I sometimes feel like it would be easier to be with the rest of them; where I didn't know any better.

I feel so hollow.

I now realize why Remy always looks so defeated. This job is more than anyone could ever handle. Even an angel.

Remy is showing me some frightening things. He told me that things will get far worse before they get better.

⚷

Today, I asked Remy why I felt like this, considering I am supposed to be a part of something so miraculous and holy and good.

He's never mentioned Christ before, until today.

He reminded me that I knew what happened at the end of His story. He made sure I hadn't forgotten the sacrifice that was made so long ago.

"The crown oppressed Him, Ansiel," he told me. "And our sins laid heavy on Him."

I couldn't comprehend.

"He didn't want this, either, Ansiel."

Remy's face grew weary.

"Then why did He do it?" I asked.

"Because He knew what it would take. He knew He had to. And so do you."

I nodded.

"Not much longer," he concluded.

⚷

The bottle of pills lay half empty on the counter.

I saw his hands shaking, violently, as he put another one to his mouth.

He took a drink of whatever the stagnant liquid was in the cup to his right.

A dark image slowly slid the bottle closer to his face; already displaying the effects of the pills. It was urging him to keep going.

I watched him helplessly as he reached into the image, picked up the bottle unsteadily and poured its contents into his mouth.

The room was eerily calm.

I stood in silent apprehension, my body numb from knowing what was about to happon. Tho darkness that I was so tired of seeing was not overwhelming this time; it was unassertive and reclusive- almost as if it knew it only had one task- one simple task to finish and then it would be satisfied.

And then I saw the note, resting there on the table- like a feather anxiously awaiting a soft wind to carry it away.

In sorrowful, scrawled handwriting, and drenched in tears, it read:

> My wish for you is to know that I never wanted anything more than peace.
>
> Please don't be angry at me; this is the only way I knew how to find it.
>
> It isn't like I never looked. Perhaps I was never meant to find it.

"No," I whispered to myself as I covered my mouth. Tears flooded my face as I watched him start to convulse and finally fall to the floor.

I wanted to turn away. I wanted to run as fast as I could and never look back.

Instead, I knelt beside him and held his head in my hands. I whispered to him how the love of God was enough. I told him stories, as he laid there, dying in my hands, about how none of us would ever be worthy. I rocked back and forth as he convulsed, screaming at him that we would *never* be enough but that didn't matter.

I screamed at him that the grace we received was sufficient. Words just kept coming from my mouth over and over and I tried to console him- as I tried to save him.

I told him where he could find *peace*.

He began to choke profusely as he rolled to his side.

It would not be long now.

He was my best childhood friend. I remember spending countless summers with him, swimming in the river behind my house. I remember playing softball for hours on end and racing him to the bus stop. I remember the mean girl on the bus who pulled my hair all year and bullied me relentlessly until he confronted her. He was the brother I never had. He watched over me and I knew I could count on him.

I looked over to Remy, who was knelt down in the kitchen. He looked at me with question in his eyes.

He was waiting for me. He was waiting on my call. We both waited for direction.

I closed my eyes again, as I listened so intently for the answer.

"Now!" I screamed into the empty room. Remy arose swiftly as the room filled with a bright light, that familiar light that I needed to see so desperately.

The room shook with a violent force.

I quickly shifted my gaze and looked deeply in my dying friend's eyes until he was able to focus on me. Seconds later, the seizing had stopped. His body was now calm. It took him just a moment to recognize me.

"Elizabeth?" he gasped, almost with fright in his eyes.

"Peace, Adam," I whispered as my tears covered his face, "is closer than you think."

From afar, I watched the paramedics arrive in just a few short minutes.

"That was a close call!" a medic shouted to him as they starting giving him oxygen in the ambulance.

I continued to watch over him from a distance and I knew this was the change he needed. I prayed a prayer that his thirst for peace would be quenched.

I saw the tears stream down his face and I heard his own prayers from the ambulance- prayers of forgiveness and mercy. He had seen me. He knew I was there.

And now he knew he could start over.

JOURNAL ENTRY

One thing I've missed since my death is human touch.

I can't begin to describe how much I yearn for it. I have no recollection of what it feels like. But then again, Remy told me this day would come. Remy reminds me that the love of God - in all its fullness- suffices here. He promises me that the amount of peace and love I will experience will surpass any amount I ever felt on earth. It will always be more than enough.

He will hold my hand from time to time because he knows I long for this interaction. Yet it isn't the same.

I hope this feeling passes soon.

I found myself walking down the middle of a busy interstate bridge- the dark blue water on both sides me.

"Ansiel."

I glanced over to see Remy beside me.

I flinched from time to time, as I felt the draft from the cars speeding by us on the tiny roadway- nervous that they would undoubtedly hit us.

Then I realized that we were already dead.

"Ansiel," Remy repeated.

I slowed my pace and looked at him with exhaustion in my eyes.

"You're letting them win, Ansiel."

How could I explain to him that I felt like I wasn't meant for this. It wasn'tlike I had a choice.

"I won't always be with you," he reminded me as he hung his head.

"I know," I replied, with a tinge of resentment in my voice.

"I want you- I *need* you to remember, Ansiel- that they will feed and thrive on the weak and vul- nerable at heart. They prey on the weak. All they know is evil. Ansiel, they're brainwashed," he said quietly as I saw tears well up in his eyes.

Remy even had compassion for our enemies.

"I promise you, it will get easier. All you will know is this life. This *place*. And then and only then will you be able to appreciate its splendor, Ansiel."

I wanted to believe him. I really did. "What are we really doing here Remy?" I questioned. I think he could sense the despair in my voice.

He looked at me with his caring eyes and took my hand. "I think it's time you see something different," he smiled.

It was dark and the air was crisp. Remy continued to hold my hand as he guided me off of the pier, and onto the dark blue water. I wondered for a moment why he was holding onto me, considering how nothing could really happen. But then again, the interaction did feel comforting. Although his touch was cold, it still felt purposeful to me.

The ocean was calm and still. It resembled a sheet of glass as far as I could see. I looked over at Remy, who had tucked away his wings and was now gently closing his eyes. He looked so feeble. I knew he was praying.

"Are you praying for me, Remy?"

"Of course," he replied quietly as he looked up. "Constantly." I knew he was telling the truth.

I stood there, hovering above the massive body of water. The feeling was surreal. There was nothing to hear except for the occasional sound of the ocean waves, crashing into the shore. The peacefulness subsided and a forceful began to blow through my hair.

"Look up, Ansiel," he whispered.

When I did, everything ceased. I had never seen anything more beautiful in my entire life. Not only was I able to see every star in the sky, but every planet. Every constellation. Every heavenly body.

I couldn't have moved if I wanted to. I felt so humble and insignificant. How could I have possibly deserved this. I felt so selfish for not wanting it in the first place.

"It's real," I heard Remy utter softly. As many times I was certain Remy had seen the same scene, he appeared speechless. "It's just so amazing every time."

This moment paled in comparison to any of my greatest memories on earth.

"Ansiel, I want you to know that you belong here. I know you don't believe that, but let me promise you that you are vital here. They need you. And I need you," he smiled.

I hugged Remy forcefully. "Thank you," I whispered to him.

JOURNAL ENTRY

Remy showed me the heavens today.

There aren't words beautiful enough to describe what I saw. I hope I remember this day forever.

If I could just show them, maybe then they would believe.

Now I really hope this *isn't* a dream. I never want to wake up. It is perfect here.

And I no longer feel alone.

11

I sat in the waiting room for what seemed like hours.

I was one of them now. From time to time, Remy would concede to my plea for this. It was good for me. But it was always an eerie feeling, being a human again. I felt so vulnerable and powerless.

It didn't make things easier, though. I still had a job to do and sometimes it made the burden even heavier.

I sat there patiently, as I waited for my next encounter.

I watched closely as an old man hobbled through the front door, struggling to keep it open with all his might. His son was holding onto his right arm as the man carefully and deliberately put one foot in front of the other. It appeared that he was in his final stages.

This had to be him, I thought to myself. He looked at me quickly and I smiled at him.

The old man slowly sat down beside me, with the aid of his son. He was out of breath and had a blank look on his face. Out of the corner of my eye, I saw him look at me again.

His demeanor toward me changed immediately. "Sarah?" His voice sounded excited yet confused.

"Dad, no.." his son interjected, preparing to correct him. I looked at the son and nodded as if to tell him it was okay. He paused curiously.

Again, I prepared my heart.

"Sarah!" he exclaimed. His grin widened and he reached in to hug me. I smiled and hugged him back.

"You're so grown up! I haven't seen you in years. How old are you now?" he questioned. His face was lit up with a glow I'd never forget.

"I'll be twenty-five soon, Grandpa," I replied, trying to hold back my tears.

"Oh, my. And your dad told me you graduated college. Is that right?"

"That's right! And I got a job and just bought my first house!" I exclaimed. I glanced over at the old man's son. He discreetly wiped the tears streaming down his face.

The old man squeezed my hand. "That's wonderful. I am so happy for you. I have been waiting for you to come see me for a long time now. But I know you have more important things to do then visit an old, boring thing like me," he laughed.

I squeezed his hand back tightly.

I did not know this man.

I did, however, know his mind. His memory had been fading rapidly, and the disease was killing him.

We chatted for a few more minutes until the nurse opened the door and called the old man up.

"Judy! Judy! This is my granddaughter! Isn't she beautiful? I'm so glad you finally get to meet her!"

The nurse looked puzzled but went along. "Yes, indeed, Mr. Anderson! She is. You have the same smile," she replied. The nurse took the old man's hand and guided him through the door.

The old man's son grabbed my arm.

I turned to him.

"I don't know who you are, but my father has been asking to see his granddaughter for three years now. She- she was my daughter." The man seemed to struggle for words. "She passed away last year in a car accident. My father has no idea."

My heart was overflowing with grief and joy at the same time.

I already knew the whole story.

"Thank you," he whispered.

The old man turned toward me once more. "Sarah, don't forget about your ol' grandpa, now, okay? I love you!" He hugged me one more, forcefully this time.

"I love you too, Grandpa," I whispered in his ear.

The old man never turned his gaze from me until the nurse gently closed the door behind him.

JOURNAL ENTRY

Remy tells me that the heart is more vital than the mind. The mind will try to rationalize and study and scrutinize.

And will eventually forsake us.

But the heart- the heart will never leave us. It will simply trust and believe. And sometimes, that's enough to go on.

⚷

I stood in the back of the parlor, silently and unnoticed, and watched as the elderly man bent down over the open casket and kissed his wife on the cheek gently, one last time.

The darkness never came.

The funeral director softly put his arm around the old man's shoulders to offer condolence. I saw their gazes meet as they both nodded in a solemn congruence.

I walked closer and sat down in the very last seat, in the very last row.

At this time, the protocol would normally be for the old man to walk away, remembering the good times they shared as he made his way to his car; his loving family waiting for him outside the door and they prepared for the journey to the cemetery.

But not this time.

The funeral director began to slowly close the lid to the casket.

"Wait," I heard the old man request of him.

I sat up in my seat.

I watched the man look longingly at his wife in the glazed oak casket, covered in white roses- a single tear rolling down his cheek. I gazed intently from my seat as he took her finger- her ring finger- and stared at her wedding band.

I stood up slowly and made my way to the front of the parlor, now standing between the two men, making certain they could not sense my presence.

"Sixty-two years," he whispered to the funeral director.

The young funeral director looked at him and smiled a quaint smile, like he was obliged to do.

"Do you have any idea what that means?" the old man asked, unexpectedly to the funeral director.

He paused for a moment, looking closely into his eyes for an answer.

"That means for sixty-two years, one woman has eaten breakfast with me, kissed me goodbye before work, raised my babies, listened to me complain, told me everything was going to be okay, prayed for me daily, told me I was good enough for her and then kissed me goodnight. She could have done anything else with her life. She could have had anyone else. But she chose me. For sixty-two years." He choked on his words.

The funeral director stood there, helpless. I'm certain he had never heard these things before.

"I lost a child, son," I heard him say. "I lost her far too soon." He began to cry harder. "This woman saved me. She gave me hope."

The old man's eyes were now welling with tears as he leaned in closer and put a firm hand on the top of the casket.

I grabbed him and hugged him tightly. I sobbed, wishing he could feel me.

When his tears ceased, I heard him whisper, "But even after everything, I still believe in His grace."

He slowly turned and walked toward the door.

I wanted to comfort him.

I prayed for a peace that I know would not come quickly.

I didn't belong here. I belonged with him. He needed me.

I felt the affliction the old man was feeling. I sensed the isolation begin to overtake him already. My heart was broken as now I felt a new kind of helplessness.

That man was my father.

I hastily scoured the funeral home for anything I could find with a date on it. I finally stumbled upon a recent newspaper on the funeral director's desk.

I wasn't sure how to feel when I read the date.

I quickly did the math.

I had been dead for fifty-four years.

Although I was no longer aware of time, this was an important day for two reasons. For one, I had just learned of the death of my mother. Secondly, I finally got some insight as to how long I had been gone.

Fifty- four years.

I felt as though I had been here for a thousand years, at least. I stood there for a moment, not sure how to react to all of this.

So this is what eternity feels like.

JOURNAL ENTRY

Today was far more beautiful than I had expected it to be.

But Remy was right when he said that it would drain me. I haven't really been tired since I've been here but I feel like I am wasting away now and I need rest.

If I could only let them know how quickly life passes. If only I could go back, just one last time.

I would tell them to look forward to their last breath, and not be afraid of it.

If only I could let them know what awaits them on the other side.

I am now skilled to understand that people deal with darkness very differently.

I've learned that the weak usually retreat- keeping to themselves and denying the pain that they can never fully avoid. And eventually, they simply agree to come to terms with what has hap- pened- and life goes on for them. But they never really heal.

My heart breaks for these.

I have seen the strong emerge triumphantly- using these trials as an opportunity to grow. They understand the reason behind their suffering.

And then there are others whose hearts remain broken and numb- and simply wait until the *light* finds them.

These are mine.

Frankie sat on the edge of his bed, twiddling a paper airplane between his fingers. He thought about how badly he wanted to grow up. Even at such a young age, he knew his purpose.

"Time for dinner," his mother smiled at him as she peeked around the door frame into his room.

Frankie looked up at her slowly and smiled back. Before he made his way downstairs, he looked longingly at the large model airplane his mother helped him assemble just a few short days ago.

Dottie was always the stubborn one. Beautiful, yet stubborn. Stubborn in a good sense, of course. Strong and outspoken.

She was the description of a true mother. She was kind, loving, compassionate. She was vibrant- and her positive, infectious personality kept her from ever meeting a stranger.

She was the epitome of *life*.

But as she lie there, so still as though she was sleeping, it wasn't her *life* on her family's mind. It was the inevitable fear of what was coming soon.

Life was fleeting. Death was upon her. And no one was prepared.

Are they ever.

Frankie and I had met just a few years before my death. Very quickly we developed a strong friendship that covered the hundreds, sometimes thousands, of miles between us.

I had never in my life met someone so enthusiastic about life. I remember how contagious his smile was and how genuine his words were; no matter what he spoke of.

I remember seeing him at my funeral. He stood in the back, alone, even though he knew nearly everyone in attendance.

I knew he was mad at me for leaving.

I tried visiting him a few times in his dreams. But he would always fight me. He would never let me in. I just wanted to tell him how happy I was here. And how sorry I was that we couldn't have remained friends longer than we were able to. I wanted him to know that I missed him and ask him not to forget about me.

⚷

Years later, I found myself in yet another hospital room. I had lost count of how many I had seen since my time here.

I had been preparing for this for some time now. Still, no amount of preparation could have equipped me for it.

I stood by Frankie and his siblings as they watched their mother fight to stay alive. I watched them weep quietly as they just stood there, waiting.

The hairs on my arms stood up as I saw the dark cloud enter the room. I hung my head. I hated this.

Frankie turned his head and looked at me solemnly. It was the first time we had seen each other in, well, as long as I could calculate.

I met his gaze. His face showed nothing but blankness.

The dark cloud quickly made its way to my best friend. I tried to hold back my tears but it was useless. The cloud, now taking on the form of a being, shrouded him.

I was not strong enough for this. I looked frantically for Remy but he was nowhere to be found.

"Can't you do something?" he said to me, exhausted and emotionless. There was evidence of tears on his cheeks. "I mean, isn't this your *job*?" he asked.

My heart sank as I realized he could see me. I reached for his hand but mine went right through it. I wanted more than anything to comfort him.

"No," I whispered through my tears.

If only he knew.

He simply turned his head back in the direction of his mother. The thick cloud had produced from it a small demon- slowly appearing from somewhere behind us, making its way toward Frankie. It grinned up in satisfaction at me.

"Frankie," I urged, fighting to hold back my sobs and wanting desperately to grab onto him. "I know you don't understand now, but you will. I promise," I begged him.

He paused for a moment and then turned back to me. "No. You're wrong. How does this possibly make sense? She's a wife. A mother. *My* mother." he demanded. His voice was bitter and now filled with anger. The darkness was forming hands around his throat.

Frankie began to choke. "How could you let this happen? You knew this was going to happen, didn't you! First you, now her!" There was hatred in his voice now.

I closed my eyes as I sobbed- and prayed for him to see what I saw.

When I finished, I looked over and saw Remy at the doorway.

"I-I can't do this, Remy," I begged him. "He will never forgive me if I do. He will hate me." I was almost screaming now, in order to for him to hear me through the thick cloud and chaotic madness that separated us.

Suddenly, I watched in awe as Remy took on a form I had never seen before. His enormous wings unfolded as he hovered- floated- over Dottie's body. The small demon shrieked when it saw this and leapt toward Remy.

My stomach churned as with a one swift move, Remy caught the demon in mid-air and violently snapped its neck. The demon fell lifeless onto the hard floor before it crumbled into ashes and slowly disappeared from sight.

Remy's violent demeanor changed instantly. "Ansiel," he said quietly to me, but still focusing on Dottie as his weightless body drifted over her-"What is your heart telling you? What is His will telling you?"

"That we have to let her go," I cried out to him. I was sobbing loudly now.

"Then that's what we must do," he confirmed softly as his wings embraced her, keeping her safely inside.

I looked around the room at her weeping family. I stood perfectly still, holding my breath as a bright light shone through the crevices in Remy's wings.

"Hold onto your friend, Ansiel. I'll do it," Remy succeeded. I grabbed onto Frankie with all of my might, making sure he knew I was right beside him. This time, I knew he could feel me.

Remy's face was distraught but so focused on nothing but Dottie. I watched him continue to hover over the young mother's body. I watched his eyes zone in on her, as he methodically breathed in and out, focusing just on the dying mother as he began to envelop her frail body.

I knew Frankie could see Remy. He wept softly and I felt him desperately squeeze my hand.

I looked hard at her weeping children and husband. With my mind, I urged them to hug her one last time. They obliged.

Frankie hugged his mother one last time and then turned back to me, burying his head in my embrace. "Now?" he cried.

"Yes," I whispered.

He slowly raised his head and focused on his dying mother as Remy wrapped his wings around her one last time. The room fell silent.

"Watch," I begged Frankie, clinging to his arm.

And then we witnessed Dottie, once feeble and tired, rise slowly from the bed. She looked at Remy and smiled at him as if they had known each other their entire lives.

Remy smiled back at her as he extended his hand to her.

"They know, don't they?" she said sweetly to Remy. "They know that I won't be gone long, don't they? Oh, how I will miss them until then."

"They do," Remy acknowledged. "We will wait for them."

Dottie gleamed at Remy as they slowly faded from sight.

⚷

Over a decade later, I sat beside Frankie in the cockpit of the small plane he had just boarded.

As he analyzed and adjusted the instruments in the machine, I saw him twiddle a small, paper airplane between his fingers as he let out a soft sigh.

For decades now, I watched my best friend struggle with the grief caused from the death of his mother.

I watched him try to end his own life- more than once. And each time, my heart broke for him. Each time, I wished he knew I was there beside him.

But this day was different. Everything changed on this day.

"I'm not mad anymore," I heard Frankie say.

As the plane ascended, I saw him smile to himself as we made our way higher and higher.

My eyes filled with tears as I saw him glance at the tattoo on his left arm that read: "I am right here with you."

He laughed. "You are, aren't you."

And the light- once dim and almost unnoticeable in the cabin of that tiny plane, was now as bright as I had ever seen.

⊶⇼

JOURNAL ENTRY

When I see them leave that old, tired place, I always get anxious.

I wonder if they'll be scared at that last moment before it happens. I've seen terror in some of their eyes.

But then other times, I see real, true peace.

I see elation.

I see *belief*.

They don't know what's coming. They don't yet understand the splendor of what the next few seconds- and then, *eternity*- hold for them.

And that's when I wait. That's when I feel complete again.

Remy was right about the notion of time here. It was like I was seeing all of this happen a hundred years too late. It is still so hard for me to make sense of.

But I guess I have to believe him when he tells me that the easiest way to handle it is to recognize that I have always been here.

JOURNAL ENTRY

I'm sitting here alone with the feeling that one of the most difficult of tasks is still before me.

I could see them long before they happened now.

I'm not sure if I'm ready to do this but Remy reminded me today that I will not fight this alone.

God, be with me.

○━╾

Evil comes in many forms.

It presents itself in the image of money, distractions, desire, success, wit and intelligence.

Evil can even come masked as happiness, beauty and hope.

It cloaks itself in the form of a friend, a confidant and sometimes- even an angel.

It comes disguised as everything you've ever wanted.

I was certain that hundreds, no- thousands- of years had gone by.

I know it didn't matter. But I asked Remy to tell me anyway.

He put his hand on my cheek, just like he did the day I died.

"What will you gain if I tell you?" he asked me. "Affirmation."

He smiled. "Okay, Ansiel."

I took a deep breath and closed my eyes as Remy pressed his hand harder.

"Two thousand years. One hundred, sixteen days."

My heart fell as I stood there, unable to move.

I had accepted that I was never going home. This was my life now. This was all I had. But there was always a small glimmer of hope in the back of my mind that this was all still a dream. Until now. Until two thousand years later.

I thought about this as Remy and I walked down the corridor of the hospital in silence, yet again. No matter who or when it was- no matter where the encounter- it was always the same hospital. Same pictures in the hallways. Same people in the waiting room. Same magazines for them to read. I could never make sense of it.

I was so tired of this place. So tired of the pain I always felt here.

But this day would prove much different than the rest.

When Remy saw this encounter in foresight, he warned me that it would not be easy and that he wasn't sure what to expect- but I knew he was feeling uneasy. He was dreading it for me.

I recognized at some point I would have to do this. I guess I was just hoping I would someday forget about it. I had avoided it for too long, and it was inevitably time.

Remy's pace slowed down as he wrung his hands nervously. Even after all this time in training, he still worried for me. He still wanted to make sure that I knew how important it was to fulfill my purpose. He knew that ultimately I was responsible for fulfilling God's will during my encounters- but I know that still made him anxious to some degree.

I glanced over at him but he did not look at me this time.

"Remy?" I suggested as I held out my hand to him. He took it reluctantly. "I'll be okay, you know? I can do this."

He smiled slightly, with his head still down, still averting my gaze.

I stopped walking and squeezed his hand firmly. "Remy. What's wrong?" I asked of him. I had never seen him this distracted.

He remained quiet but then finally looked up at me with tears in his eyes.

I became concerned.

"Ansiel," he said softly, "It's your last one."

"What?" I replied, confused.

"It's your last one," he repeated solemnly, with an emotionless face. He squeezed my hand back and I saw a small tear fall from his eye.

My heart fell. How could this be? In essence, I hadn't been here long at all.

"Are you sure?" I asked him.

He paused for a moment, still looking at me thoughtfully.

"Yes."

"But, Remy- what does that mean?" I asked.

"I don't know, Ansiel. No one really knows what happens at this point," he replied softly. "It's different for all of us." He dropped his head again.

I had no idea what to say or feel.

"I'm not sure if I'll see you again, Ansiel."

My heart stopped.

"Romy no."

"Ansiel," he replied, "You must hear me. They will try their best to stop you. They want you as theirs. They know this is your breaking point."

I looked down but slowly nodded my head in approval- although I was in utter disbelief.

I took a deep breath.

"Ansiel…you have to," he reminded me.

"I know," I confirmed.

"Look to Him for guidance. He will direct you, Ansiel. Remember what you've learned."

He hugged me tightly as we stood there in silence for several moments. I held onto him for as long as I could. I knew he wouldn't let go of me until I was ready. Somehow I found comfort in that.

For the first time, I felt warmth radiating from Remy's body. It was the best feeling in the world.

With tearful eyes, I ever so slowly loosened my grip.

The heart rate monitor was beeping obnoxiously. I looked at the tangled web of tubes and wires attached to him as he lie there helplessly. There were too many of them to count. The knotted wires reminded me of my own state of confusion and discontent when I was with him. I would always try to unravel them; to find out the secrets and lies that lived within them, but the web had no end.

Beep. Beep. Beep.

The sterile smell of the room was overwhelming to my senses.

I looked down at the man, now in his old age. The wrinkles on his face were deeper now than ever. The sallow, dark circles under his eyes reminded me of how empty I felt when I was with him; how hollow he once made me feel. His eyes had always made me feel so unwanted. To me, he still looked like the epitome of betrayal. He was the hate that consumed me.

Beep. Beep.

Without warning, a large demon gracefully floated out from the wall and stood silently near the edge of the bed.

He was different than the rest. He stood tall, dressed in a cloak; a dark hood pulled over his face. He appeared to be more in the image of a man than the demons I had grown accustomed to.

He did not move from his haunting position; he simply tilted his head slightly and examined the old man.

I watched him cautiously as I felt the hairs on my neck stand up. The room already felt so lifeless and void.

Abruptly, he turned his head in my direction.

The demon had no face.

His black, shadowy hands tapped the rail on the old man's bed as he continued to direct his attention on me.

Tap, tap, tap.

He was one of the most horrible demons I had seen. I remember seeing him once in my nightmares.

I did my best to not look at him.

Beep.

"This is what you want, Ansiel." The demon's voice was deep and rattling.

"No," I replied meekly.

"I will make it painless," he stated. "Your job is done here."

Beep. Beep.

I looked over at the machines. Every beep was a secret. Every beep was a lie and broke my heart once more.

The repetitive noises from the machine were now farther and farther apart. It was happening. I could feel it. I could feel the attraction between this figure and the man in the bed. It was a perfect combination of evil intent and triumph.

The demon glided closer to the head of the bed as the lights in the room flickered twice and then went off completely.

The beeping stopped.

I looked up, knowing that Remy was in the room, watching me closely. His face was so distorted as he focused on the demon a hair's breath away from me. I could barely make him out in the dying light of the room.

He was waiting on me to change my mind.

So was I.

I once loved him.

When we were married, I would pack his lunch every day. And every day, I would put a note inside his lunchbox that simply read: "I love you."

I did this every, single day without fail. Even when I was tired or sick or angry- I still got up at 4:30 in the morning to write that stupid note. I was intent on making sure he knew. I did not want our marriage to become a statistic.

He had a rough childhood. I often wept for him in the middle of the night because I knew that he never completely believed me when I told him I would never abandon him. I promised him I would never treat him the way others had.

We would stay up late sometimes and vow to not make our children pay for our mistakes in life. We would talk about our failures and how we had overcome them. We would be there for each other no matter what.

So when I discovered that he had been having an affair, I didn't confront him at first. I wanted to see if his conscience would get to him.

I wanted him to tell me himself.

And so I waited. For almost six months.

During that time, I started putting different notes in his lunch box. Notes that read: "How could you do this to me?" and "I don't love you anymore."

I could not believe this was happening. Not to me. This couldn't be my life. I was pregnant with our first baby. We were newlyweds. This wasn't how it was supposed to work.

I stayed up weeping every night for a different reason now. He heard my cries. Yet he did nothing.

After some time, I realized the hard truth. He had stopped reading my notes a long time ago. He would come home and say nothing about the new notes because he hadn't read any of them. He had no idea that I even knew.

I remember the pain and discourse I went through after that. For years, I did my best to deal with it. For years, it haunted me. My life was in shambles. And although I quickly realized that he was not at all who I thought he was, the fact that he had gone to great measures to convince me otherwise, made me feel so stupid and naive.

All I wanted was revenge. I wanted him to feel exactly how he made me feel.

I dragged around such heavy, unbreakable chains for nearly three years after this. Anything I did or said was influenced by my imprisonment of what I thought defined me now. I knew I would never break free.

I also knew that I needed to forgive him. I knew that this was the expectation of me. Yet I never did. I would rather *die* than have him think I was okay with what he did to me.

⊙—ᴋ

I looked down as I felt something angrily claw-
ing at my feet. Two more small demons smiled back
up at me with their intimidating grins. I ignored
them- remaining still, yet I felt as though I was
about to be defeated once more.

The darkness was so overwhelming. It was thick
and had created a wall between us that could
not be penetrated. The room filled with a chaotic
noise; like the sound a television would make when
filled with static. I had never experienced this
before during an encounter. A heavy wind began to
blow through the room, dispersing papers from the
bedside table.

I strained to look at Remy. It was blurry, but
I was able to see an image of him with his head
down, and again wringing his hands. I knew he was
praying for me.

The faceless figure was still tapping on the
bedrail. His head still tilted slightly, waiting
for my acknowledgement.

"I could use him," he said in a calm tone, as
a grotesque, black, bony finger grazed the old
man's arm.

For a moment, I thought this was the end. I wanted
to give up. This could have been my revenge. This
would have made me feel justified for what he
did to me, to my family. I could have shaken him
awake- I could have looked into his untruthful
eyes and told him that he was about to get what he
deserved. And that no one would miss him.

The faceless demon was now hovering over his body; his long cloak covering him like a blanket.

The vengeance was overpowering me as the dark cloud in the room got even darker, swirling around as if it were a tornado about to devastate an entire city.

"Painless," his grim voice reminded me. "And he will never know it was you."

I remember crying myself to sleep one night, only to find him shaking me violently. I arose disoriented. I woke up to him- his eyes looking through me. "Go pray to your stupid God," he said to me. "Maybe He will save you," he mocked me.

With that memory, my anger began to surface again. I heard the demons laugh over the loudness of the room.

Remy had dropped to his knees, sobbing. I could barely see him.

The room was nearly pitch black now.

As he lie there, his shallow breaths shaking his entire body, I wanted nothing more than to use my last save on someone else. Someone more worthy. He didn't deserve this.

The other demons were latched to me. My stomach churned as I felt the excruciating pain of one of the demons lacerating my legs.

Memories kept flooding my mind of how he had abandoned me. Using the faint glow of the light from a lamp post outside the window, I stared at him blankly, waiting for a sign that I didn't have to go through with this. That I didn't have to forgive him. I owed him nothing. I looked down only to see drops of my own blood on the demons' claws and mouths.

But the feeling became more and more prevalent. I was consumed with guilt. *Me.*

As I had seen many times before, a fleet of nurses ran hastily into the room from the hallway.

I heard Remy weep from across the room. He stood up abruptly as I fumbled to the hospital bed. Everything had become hazy and I felt as though the darkness had taken something out of me.

But with a racing heart, I quickly reached behind his hospital bed and pulled the plug from the outlet.

I studied him for a moment as he took a deep gasp.

Sobbing and exhausted, I asked God to breathe new life into him again.

Immediately, the lights came back on and the nurses scurried to the bed in confused states. I looked at him, lying there in the bed, and watched as the color returned to his face. I saw his eyelashes flutter and he began to breathe on his own.

The faceless monster charged at me.

But it was too late.

The darkness was clearing now.

With tears still streaming down my face, I slowly turned and left the room.

14

The bitter cold air cut my face like a newly sharpened blade as I walked down the crowded streets of the city I once loved. The wind was blowing violently from every direction as the hoard of people frantically tried to escape the elements.

Their faces were somber and sedative. It was as though the darkness had enveloped the entire city. They were purposeless. I remember how vibrant this place used to be; how energetic. But now it was nothing but desolate and forgotten.

I listened intently to their thoughts. Some were walking slowly, planning their evening with their families. But even still, their thoughts of discontent and worry were far more apparent.

I continued to watch, undetected, as the mass of those passing by scrambled to their cars to join the rush hour traffic. They seemed so distracted. Person after person—*emotionless.*

"What has happened to them?" I asked God aloud.

I sat down on a bench at a congested intersection, observing for a few more minutes before I arose and started to make my way to where I had been instructed to go. Remy had warned me to be ready for anything on this visit, making it more unnerving than normal.

A chill went down my spine as I realized I was standing in the very spot where I had been killed. I looked around for Remy.

And then I remembered what had just occurred.

Determined to figure out my destiny from here on out, I continued walking, looking into the eyes of everyone I passed, hoping someone would notice me. Remy told me that every now and then, someone with spiritual eyes would be able to make contact with us. I was aching for some type of human contact- if only for a few seconds.

It was so cold- abnormally cold for this time of year. The homeless were scurrying to their make-shift tents on the sidewalk, just to try to escape the brutal sting of the wind that had just picked up. I put my head down, walking quickly, but still very cognizant of listening for my instructions.

When I finally looked up, I noticed a small girl, perhaps five or six, about twenty feet ahead of me. She was tip-toeing carefully along the curb. I stood there for a moment, entranced by the young girl. I watched her intently as she cautiously put one foot in front of the other, steadying herself with her arms out to her sides as though she was walking a tightrope.

Occasionally, she would reach back and adjust her backpack to help keep her balance.

Her light brown hair covered one side of her face and her pale blue eyes never once drifted from her path. She was oblivious to the chaos around her.

I saw her smile to herself, still ignoring the commotion of the traffic and flood of people. She was content. I studied her as she focused on her next step.

She reminded me a lot of my younger self.

Traffic was picking up now and I saw who I assumed was the young girl's father, a man about my age, snatch her up quickly from behind. The girl's father was even more alluring. He was tall, with the same light brown hair and striking, even lighter blue eyes. I saw the man glance in my direction as they started walking more hastily. I watched as he raised the hood of her coat and pulled her in closer to him.

Then the man met my gaze and began to stare at me as if he could see me. As if he was trying to figure something out. Could he see me? I wondered. My anticipation started to build. I remember the instance of the old man in the hospital bed.

The man, gripping the small girl tightly, grinned at me.

I stopped abruptly and leered back at him, hoping this was not an illusion. The young girl was still minding her own business, looking down at her shoes while her father finally loosened his grip on her. His pace quickened once more but this time his warm expression faded.

Traffic was swirling dangerously by us now as the gap began to close between us. They were zooming by at incredulous speeds, just inches away.

And then I watched in horror as the man stared blankly at me and tossed the girl into the busy road.

In less than a second, I heard the young girl scream, tires screech and horns blow.

And then a sickening, loud thud.

"NO!" I screamed as I lunged into the traffic. My heart was racing and I felt ill.

The man intercepted me forcefully.

I realized something had gone terribly wrong.

The sky turned a dark black and the temperature outside rose almost immediately. The wind was destructive now; blowing debris into the air, making it difficult to see anything. The thick clouds rotated, forming numerous funnels in the evening sky. The climate had transformed from a blistery, winter day into an uneasy feeling of an approaching tornadic storm.

I suddenly felt a second hard blow to my chest as the man viciously threw me to the ground.

I tried fighting back but his hold on me was too firm.

"You can't save everyone!" he hissed in my ear, with his cold hands around my neck.

I gasped.

A demon.

I had no time to respond, as my eyes begain to cloud up from the pressure he had around my throat.

I looked up at him in terror. His once soft eyes were now a burning red. I winced as his hands dug deeper into my neck.

"You will not win!" he hissed again as his gripped tightened once more.

He can't kill you, I reminded myself. He can't hurt you. My mind was racing as I struggled to breathe now.

"No, I can't," I heard the demon whisper. "But I can make you mine."

I looked back into his glowing, sinister eyes as I tried desperately to take a breath.

Then everything went black.

I slowly opened my eyes to see a rat scurry across the cold, stone floor, mere inches from my face. Disoriented, I closed my eyes tightly and tried opening them again. As I strained to regain my focus, I heard a loud creak from somewhere in the dark room.

As the door slowly opened, a faint light poured over me.

From the light, I was able to make out a small dungeon cell; I was lying in the middle of it. The floor was cold and wet and the stones comprising it were covered in dirt and mold.

My heart dropped as Iheard the sound of metal clanging on metal.

I then realized that I was chained.

I sat up from my vulnerable position and sobbed into my hands.

"Don't even attempt to move," I heard an evil, low voice whisper. The sound of it sent chills down my spine.

I froze and held my breath.

My hands. Something was terribly wrong.

My hands were warm.

I choked in horror again.

I was human.

And then, from the doorway, entered the most horrendous, grotesque demon I had ever seen. His horns protruded from his forehead some eight inches on both sides. His eyes were an opaque white and I couldn't tell if he could even see me.

His face was covered in scars and dried blood. It was as if I was looking at the face of Satan himself.

The demon sauntered closer to me, as I tried to inch my way back, closer to the wall; as though it would offer any sort of protection from him.

The closer he got to me, the more terrified I became. His eyes were so sinister. To intimidate me even more, he opened his mouth slowly, revealing a long, forked tongue. He stood some seven feet tall and his presence alone was terrorizing. I was certain that one wrong move on my part would be my demise.

I wanted to scream for help when I suddenly remembered that I had seen him in my dreams when I was still alive. Everything about him was the same. From his dirty, sharp fingernails to the scars on his marred, scaly chest.

Again, I knew this had to all be a dream.

"Remy will not save you this time. And neither will your God," he seethed in my direction. "You belong to me now," he taunted. He was inches from my face.

He examined me up and down once more, as I continued my attempt at furthering myself from him.

"Pathetic," he said as he ran his sharp fingernails now the side of my cheek. I gritted my teeth in repulsion.

"You really thought you would *elude* me!" His voice was more threatening and demeaning now. He began to laugh, flicking his revolting tongue in and out.

"What do you want," I countered breathlessly.

The demon moved in closer and looked scornfully at me and laughed, rearing his head back. I stood firm in my place, trying my best not to fold under him, although I felt more defeated than ever before.

"Remy," the beast grinned voraciously.

"No," I instinctively retorted.

The demon snorted. "He doesn't want you. It's all a game to him. And you?" he laughed again. "You are just his *pawn*."

I knew he was lying to me. "You're wrong," I retaliated.

Even if he were right, I had no idea where to find Remy now. The thought of that made me sick to my stomach.

"You're much more powerful than Remy," he persuaded me. "He will soon realize that and then he'll be rid of you, you know. That's been his plan all along." He blinked his cloudy eyes as he lingered closely to my shaking body.

"What do you mean, 'rid' of me?" I questioned him.

"Ah, he has you so fooled," the demon mocked. He leaned in even closer now and whispered in my ear. "He hasn't told you? You are his replacement."

I was confused but continued to listen to his explanation.

"Why do you think he's training you so diligently, Ansiel," he hissed at me again.

My thoughts were jumbled by his words. They somehow made sense to me.

"Where is he," I demanded of demon with confidence. He laughed at me in retort.

"Where is my friend!" I commanded once more as I started to charge him, determined on breaking free.

"Your friend?" he snapped back at me. "He was once one of us. Didn't he tell you that? He is not here, you foolish girl," he snapped back at me. "But when I *find* him? You will be of no more concern. He will easily give you up in order to save himself."

I sat there in horror at his words. How could this be?

"Bring him to me. And I will give you my word that I will set you free. *Free*, Ansiel. Back where you belong."

My mind was racing. Did he mean *home*?

"No more disconnect. No more trying to find your purpose. Back home with your family. Your old life. You would like that, wouldn't you?"

The mere thought of that chance took my breath away.

The demon hunkered down slightly, appearing vulnerable.

"More time with them to finish what you started. They have missed you. And you would pick up right where you left off. Doesn't that sound…. perfect?" he smiled slyly.

I could not respond.

"It's you or him, Ansiel. You are *nothing* to him. Consider your pardon."

The demon turned abruptly and exited the room, closing the heavy prison door gently behind him as I sobbed, staring at the shackles that bound my ankles.

Remy had promised me that they could not hurt me. Was the demon telling me the truth? My mind was racing. Remy *had* been distant lately. But even so, why would he spend so much time with me if he knew about this?

My thoughts ran rampant until I drifted off to sleep.

When I awoke, I was certain that I had slept most of
the night. But the dim light of dusk that filtered
in from the barricaded window suggested it had
only been a short time. Maybe even mere minutes.

What was this place. I needed out of here. I
needed to go home.

"Remy," I called out quietly into the darkness.
"Where are you?" I begged.

I would have given anything to look into his
safe, brown eyes once more.

"Please," I pleaded again through my tears.
"Please tell me you haven't forgotten about me,"
I whispered.

I got up on my knees slowly and inched my way
backward in hopes of finding some support on the
dungeon wall. I sat, cross-legged, rocking back and
forth to console myself. I was so exhausted.

I held my head in my hands and continued to
sob quietly as I thought about what the demon had
offered me. Was he telling me the truth? It sounded
so appealing and hopeful.

A loud banging noise on the bars of the cell
startled me.

"Silence!" I heard an evil voice command in
my direction.

I hushed myself and waited until I was certain he had made his way past my cell and down
the corridor.

I sat up suddenly as I felt a heavy presence
cover my mouth. Terrified, I looked over my shoulder.

Remy. It was him.

"Remy!" I gasped.

"Shhhh, Ansiel. Please. Be very quiet," he warned as he helped me sit up carefully.

"Remy! How did they get me here? How did you find me?" I cried out to him.

"Ansiel, please," he whispered directly. "Stay quiet. I'm so sorry. I just need you to cooperate."

"But Remy, they are looking for *you*," I said

"Ansiel, I want you to listen to me very carefully. That was not supposed to happen. I need you to pay attention, okay? Pay close attention," he instructed.

I nodded ferociously in agreement. I was so glad to see his face.

He held me sternly by the shoulders.

"They said they wanted *you*, Remy," my shaky voice exclaimed.

"I know," he replied. "They're lying, Ansiel. They captured you because they knew I would come for you. They want us both."

"Why?" I whispered in disbelief.

"Ansiel, I've neglected to tell you this before now because I wasn't sure you were ready. But after your last encounter, I think it's time I explain something."

I inched closer to him, intent on not missing a word.

"I will only be here, in this place, for a little while longer. I can't tell you where I'm going, Ansiel. But when I leave, I'm leaving everything to you."

I stared at him in disbelief. The demon was telling me the truth.

"I've been training you for a long time now. I see things in you that I've never seen in any of the other protectors. And so do they," he said as he looked toward my cell door. "They know your strengths. But they also know your weaknesses. They want you on their side, Ansiel. And they will have the power to convince you that you belong there with them. But Ansiel, one thing they don't realize is how powerful you are. Do you remember when we first met and I told you that you job would be the most important? Ansiel, you were chosen to be the new leader," he said as he forced a smile.

Everything was finally adding up.

"You have to tell them the truth, Ansiel. You have to use the authority you have inside you to defeat them. They don't know what you're capable of. You must play their games, Ansiel."

In a hazy state, I opened my eyes to the sound of the prison door creaking open. Remy had disappeared into a dark corner of the room, as still as could be.

It was the same demon.

"The clock is ticking, Ansiel."

I stared at him.

"You have little time left to tell us where your friend is. And let me remind you, hell is nothing that you'll ever get used to. Let me show you."

I watched in terror as visions and images and the most nightmarish illusions danced on the chamber walls. There were bodies and fire; eyes and nothingness. They were floating around me; almost as though I could reach out and touch them. Their desperate screams nauseated me, as they begged for help. They agonized over their thirstiness.

I was sick and faint at the sight of it.

"Are you ready now?" he asked me.

"No," I proclaimed.

He lurched closer to me, flicking his tongue out while his blank eyes rolled back into his head.

"What about… now?" he asked. I shook as he held out his ghastly palm- and everyone I had ever loved- my family, my *daughter-* hovered over it. And without so much as a flinch, I watched their bodies crumble in ashes, forming a pile in his hand.

He blew the ashes into the air.

"No," I begged wearily, as I struggled to breathe.

I was suffocating.

I stared into the eyes of the demon, now sitting on my chest.

"One more chance, Ansiel," he seethed.

I began to pray as he wrapped his hands forcefully around my throat. I prayed out loud for the demon himself.

"Stop!" he shrieked as he squeezed tighter.

I knew I would die soon, but I continued asking God to save the monster who was trying to enslave me.

As he gripped me even tighter, he lifted my head off the floor, only to mercilessly slam it back down again on the solid stone.

I heard a loud crack and the familiar feeling of warm blood escaping my ears.

Disoriented and fading quickly, I said to him, "Go ahead. Try to destroy me."

He hissed violently at me, piercing his sharp claws into my neck once more.

And with my last breath, I whispered, "Because no matter how hard you try," I smiled tauntingly back at him, "We both know how this ends."

With one final shriek, I watched as the monster spontaneously burned in front of my eyes; his blackened ashes covering me.

15

I looked around to find myself in what felt like an enchanted forest; something from a fairytale.

The warmth of the sun's rays was beating down on me through the tall fir trees. It was like I had just stepped into another world. The mossy ground was soft under my feet. It all felt oddly familiar to me. The wind started to pick up gently and I looked at the narrow path that was set before me.

And then I heard it.

The bell.

My heart sank. I would never forget that sound. The bell was ringing exactly as it did the day I died.

I started to run madly toward the sound.

I ran for what seemed like hours. Days.

I didn't know where I was headed. I just knew I had to get to the old man again. I looked to Remy for help but I remembered I was now on my own.

"Keep going," I heard a voice say. It sounded so familiar.

It sounded like a father.

I ran as fast as I could. The sound of the bell was dying quickly.

I heard footsteps behind me. Something was chasing me.

"Don't look back, Ansiel," the voice said firmly, yet was so calm.

I began to run faster.

Weary and almost lifeless, I stumbled and nearly fell to the ground.

I scrambled frantically, forcing myself up and continued sprinting toward the sound of the bell. The footsteps were gaining on me.

"Keep going," the voice beckoned. "It's not much further."

My body trembled as I tried to find the strength to go on.

"You're almost there, Ansiel."

And then I saw him.

The old man from the garden on the day I died.

"Elizabeth! Hurry!" the old man shouted to me. His voice was not the one I had been hearing.

It was like everything around us was a haze; the only thing I could see clearly was the urgency in the old man's eyes.

"Run, Elizabeth! *Run!*"

Panicked, I ran as fast as I could. He was holding something out for me.

"Don't stop, now," the voice reminded me, sounding so unruffled- even through the chaos.

When I finally approached him, my knees like rubber, I saw what he had been holding for me.

It was the bell. The same bell that rang for me on the day I died.

He was stretching his arm as far as he could. I was inches from him now.

"Hurry!" he screamed once more, as the bell was finally within my reach.

"Take it," the voice suggested tranquilly.

And instinctively, I grabbed it.

TO BE CONTINUED.

T. Jane Palmer (back cover model) is a novelist and author for hire from North Vernon, Indiana. She graduated from Indiana University and Marian University.

She enjoys kayaking, college basketball, traveling, reading, writing and spending quality time with her young daughter, Finley.

She has written and published several works including her previous novel, Remembering Mary Jane (2011).

To contact Tamara regarding her author for hire availability, please email: authortjanepalmer@gmail.com

Other contact info:
Website: www.tjanepalmer-author.com
IG: TJANEPALMER
Twitter: @tamarajane84

Chris Kamrada (cover model) is a professional drummer from Orlando, Florida. He is a current member of Saints of Valory and Before You Exit. He is also the founding member of the band There for Tomorrow.

Contact info:
Website: chriskamrada.com
IG & Twitter: ckamrada

REGARDS

Chris Kamrada
James Lano Photography
Aaron Paul Wood / Dark Phoenix Productions, LLC
Mikey Webb Photography
Angie English Photography
Lily Curry
Wes Rowlett
Ayden Foga
Sam Hunter
Frankie Dessuit
Matt Kubacki
The Megel Family
Kelsey Finch

CPSIA information can be obtained
at www.ICGtesting.com
Printed in the USA
LVOW04s0056221016
509645LV00011B/174/P